Seduction Island

Touch the Sea Series, Volume 1

Autumn Gaze

Published by Dark Shadow Publishing, 2022.

This is a work of fiction. Similarities to real people, places, or events are entirely coincidental.

SEDUCTION ISLAND

First edition. November 30, 2022.

Copyright © 2022 Autumn Gaze.

Written by Autumn Gaze.

Also by Autumn Gaze

Department of Defense Series
Dead Ahead
Blue Falcon
Joint Service
Indirect Attack

Touch the Sea Series
Seduction Island

Wicked Fates Series
Beautiful Darkness
Twisted Darkness
Wicked Darkness

Watch for more at www.autumngaze.com.

Copyright 2022 By Autumn Gaze

TOUCH THE SEA BOOK ONE
Seduction island
bestselling author
autumn gaze

Seduction Island Blurb

You cannot escape the reality of tomorrow by evading it today...

Ethan Mitchell flees New York to Oahu to escape a family scandal. He doesn't want to be a part of it. He ends up meeting Ava Hunt, the woman who owns the rental house he is staying at.

The two end up being friends despite a frosty beginning. She agrees to show him around the island to places the rest of the world doesn't get to see. They hook up, and he thinks he might change his mind about bachelorhood.

She thinks he might be the one despite not looking for love.

Touch the Sea Series

Book 1 – Seduction Island
Book 2 – Gentle Rhythm
Book 3 – Dancing on Waves
Book 4 – Stormy Waters
Book 5 – Tempting the Ocean

Find Autumn Gaze:

Autumn Gaze Newsletter:
https://www.autumngaze.com/sign-up
Autumn Gaze Facebook Page:
https://www.facebook.com/AutumnGazeAuthor
Autumn Gaze Website:
http://www.autumngaze.com

Want to read more...
For **FREE?**
Sign up for Autumn's newsletter
And she'll send you updates on new releases, ARC copies of books
and a whole lotta fun!
Sign up for news and updates!
https://www.autumngaze.com/sign-up[1]

---

1. https://l.facebook.com/l.php?u=https%3A%2F%2Fwww.autumngaze.com%2Fsign-up%3Ffb-clid%3DIwAR19Pln3ibiSJ3sbPjqwZi2C2ouEk0HNj3WPfqfFHOACbgTxP-nyPseA8z2I&h=AT2zXnGSz1iKPMdJCv3D1jaSfPpsk9GF78_lcDB8lQuthwcLpds-du_0dX1lpDVC_R_aw9eie2R8y7wQzGrIpKgoi-6TEh8H8t1IcDKGEJ-NzgaLtedWWgkAd-PDYhWUrxkU

Chapter One

Ethan

"Sir."

I heard the soft voice, but I ignored it. I didn't want to leave the quiet nothingness of sleep. I didn't move a single muscle. I didn't change my breathing. Nothing. I hoped the person disturbing my very peaceful sleep would move along.

"Mr. Mitchell." The voice was a little louder, and I felt a soft hand on my arm near my wrist.

I stayed still. There was no way we were already at our destination. If she was trying to wake me up to ask if I wanted a drink, I was going to be pissed.

"Ethan," she said loud and clear.

My eyes popped open. If we were falling out of the sky, I supposed I wanted to see the Pacific Ocean coming at me. "Yes?" I asked, immediately awake and alert.

"We're landing," the flight attendant said softly.

I rubbed my face. Apparently, I had slept longer than I thought. "Thank you."

I sat the chair up and lifted the window shield to watch the descent. I felt my stress melt away. Crystal clear blue water stretched out below. The blue water contrasted with the lush green that covered the island. Oahu. I needed the ocean and the sand. I needed warmth. I wanted to be somewhere that allowed me to move about without anyone knowing who I was. I needed to be far from my family. From New York.

The private plane dropped in altitude. The green faded to tall buildings covering every inch. Houses and hotels created a barrier along the shoreline. It wasn't exactly the seclusion I'd thought I wanted, but I hoped it was enough for me to get some peace. I'd considered renting an island retreat for myself, but then I remembered I liked food and the ability to run to the store to get things.

The flight attendant returned to take a seat next to mine. She buckled her seatbelt and looked over at me. "How long are you staying in Hawaii?" she asked.

"I'm not sure," I answered. "Couple weeks. A month. I'm not sure."

"Are you fleeing the cold in New York?" she laughed. "I would love to be able to stay. It's so beautiful. I love it when we get charters here."

"Something like that," I said and looked out the window.

"I was surprised to see your name on the manifesto," she said. "I know who you are. I thought you had your own private jet."

"I do. I chose not to have my own jet fly me here because I didn't wish to be followed. People have all those tracking apps and stuff. It's obnoxious. I've got people bitching I fly too much. People wait for me at the airport to ask me to donate to this or that or accuse me of who knows what. Sometimes, a guy wants to be alone."

"Ah." She smiled brightly. "You're hiding out. I can understand why. Your company is huge. I bet you can't go anywhere without being hounded. I've watched some of the speeches you've given. You're very good. People would follow you anywhere."

"And they do," I said with a heavy sigh. Sometimes, being rich and powerful was not all it was cracked up to be.

"Maybe you just need someone to run interference for you." She grinned. "Act as a distraction."

"Or I put on my Yankees hat and sunglasses and go undercover."

I knew what she was doing. She wasn't the first woman to look at me and decide I would make a nice husband or doting boyfriend. It wasn't me she was looking at. It was the name and the money. Maybe I was jaded. I doubted it. Unfortunately for the pretty brunette, I just didn't have the energy to mess around with anyone. Even if she was very easy to look at. Even if I could probably spend one very glorious night with her. I wasn't in the mood.

"Are you going to be meeting someone here?" she asked.

The plane touched down, bounced, and then coasted across the runway. "No," I replied.

"We'll be in town a couple days," she said. "If you need someone—"

I cut her off before she could embarrass herself. "I'm here for the solitude," I told her. "I'm going to relax. Alone. I need some downtime."

I saw the moment she got the message loud and clear. I didn't want to be a dick, but I really wasn't interested. "I hope you get some rest," she said with a tight smile.

"Thank you."

I probably would have taken her up on her offer if the circumstances were different. I knew it was bad when I didn't want to hook up for a night of fun with a beautiful woman. I had to get my head straight.

Once the plane came to a full stop, I got to my feet. I was a little overdressed in my tailored suit for a vacation in Hawaii, but I didn't want anyone to see me and think I was going somewhere warm. I was running away. I wasn't trying to leave any breadcrumbs, which was why I'd booked the flight in the company name. People could be a little stalkerish. It wouldn't be hard to track my personal jet and follow me to Hawaii.

I grabbed my briefcase and walked off the plane. My bags were immediately fetched by one of the airport employees. "Mr. Mitchell?" the young man asked.

"Yes." I nodded.

"We've got your car waiting," he said and pulled my heavy suitcase across the tarmac. He hooked the garment bag with my suits over his shoulder.

I followed behind him with my sunglasses firmly in place. I'd gone from a dark, cloudy New York to a bright and sunny climate. The humidity was no joke. In the distance, I could see storm clouds. I had been to Hawaii many times. I knew the rain could come out of nowhere. It rained and then it was gone, and the sun was back high in the sky. I hoped that was the case today. I needed sun.

"Should I load your bags?" he asked eagerly.

"Yes, please," I answered. I knew he was angling for a big tip. I was happy to give it to him. "I'm going to get the keys."

"I've got them right here," he said.

I wasn't sure how I felt about that. I hoped like hell he had not decided to take the Porsche out for a spin. I had rented the car from a private dealer. I wanted freedom with a side of luxury. I was planning on a trip around the island with the top down and the sun on my head. It had been too long since I had gotten to drive anywhere.

He popped the trunk and put my suitcase inside. It barely fit. When he attempted to put my garment bag in the trunk, I stopped him. "That can go in the backseat," I said.

"Of course." He nodded.

He insisted on doing it. He handed me the key, and I gave him a hundred-dollar bill. "Thank you," he said with a grin. "Anything else you need, I'm your guy!"

"Thanks," I said. "I think I've got it from here."

He gave me an enthusiastic wave and rushed back to the building. I took off my suit jacket and tossed it into the passenger seat before sliding behind the wheel. I pulled out my phone and pulled up the address for the rental house. On the website, it looked perfect. It was one of the few properties on a couple of acres. It was secluded. I had gone back and forth between renting a house on the beach or something out of the way. I could see the beach any day. I needed the privacy.

GPS put me at the house in forty minutes. I started the engine and listened to the purr. I put it in gear and pulled out of the parking lot. I hadn't been driving for more than five minutes when the sky opened up and drenched the world around me.

It was perfect for my current mood. Despite the rain, it was still beautiful. I remembered the many happier times that had brought me to the island. My family and I had visited Hawaii many times. When I was in my teens, my friends and I convinced my parents to let us have our own summer vacation. Those were the good days. Days without the weight of the world on my shoulders. Ever since I had been moved into the CEO position, my life was nothing but meetings and numbers.

And now scandal.

I sped up the windshield wipers to try and keep up with the down-pour. My route to the house was winding with hairpin curves and a cliff on one side. If I pushed the Porsche any faster, it was almost a guar-antee I would lose control. I would spin out and possibly go flying off the cliff. Given the Porsche was a shade bigger than a tin can, surviving would be pretty unlikely. I wanted to run from the bullshit at home, but I didn't want to die. I would get through this. It was going to be brutal, but I would survive. I just hoped the company did without any major hits to our bottom line. There was nothing I could do about the reputation. It was going to take a hit no matter what I did.

I whipped around the corner, the back end slipping a little but my years of driving like a bat out of hell kicked in. I was able to pull it out of a spin and prevent myself from meeting an untimely death. I told myself to slow down, but I couldn't resist the urge to hit the gas. The adrenaline made me feel alive. The car hopped sideways as I took an-other sharp turn.

My phone started ringing. I had almost forgotten it was on. I glanced down at the screen out of sheer habit. That was all it took. When I looked up at the road, I was heading into a sharp right turn way too fast.

"Fuck!"

My heart stopped. Adrenaline wasn't what I was feeling. It was sheer terror. All thoughts of wanting to just go off the edge vanished. I wanted to live. I wanted to see the ocean. I wanted to sleep in late and drink coffee on the deck of the house I'd rented. I shifted down, knowing I would only make it worse if I slammed on the brakes. I slowed down, got into the corner, and accelerated to drive myself out of the danger. I was in the oncoming traffic lane and dangerously close to the edge. A flash of light ahead of me stopped my heart again.

"Fuck me," I groaned. I shifted down once again, lurching the car and easing back into my lane. I managed to get out of the wrong lane seconds before the oncoming car passed by me with the driver laying on the horn and flipping me the bird.

I didn't really blame the guy. I had come within seconds of killing both of us. The close call was enough to get me to slow down. It had been a stupid move. I listened to the instructions from the GPS and found my way to the driveway I had seen in the listing. The car wasn't really meant for the muddy road leading up to the house. The Porsche might not have been the best idea.

I didn't know if any of this was the right plan. I got out of New York because I didn't want to deal with the bullshit. I was exhausted. I had to make a change in my life or I really was going to drive off a cliff. I was thirty-seven and felt like I was going on eighty. My life was passing me by, and I had nothing to show for it except money. I was successful and wealthy, but I could honestly say I wasn't happy. I was a consummate bachelor. I didn't even realize just how lonely I was until the other day when I felt my world closing in and I had no one to talk to. No one even knew I was gone. My life was unfulfilling. I didn't know if I needed a woman or just a change. I hoped my time in Hawaii would help me figure out what I needed.

Chapter Two

Ava

"Kyle!" I called out the name on the side of the cup. "Caramel macchiato!"

A man that was obviously a tourist stepped up to the counter. "Mahalo," he said with a grin, as if he was fluent in the local dialect.

I moved on to the next drink order. It was a typical afternoon at the coffee shop. Unfortunately, it wasn't a great day for tips. I poured the coffee over the ice in the cup and squirted in chocolate syrup.

"Holly!" I called out the next name.

It wasn't a glamourous job, but it helped pay the bills. All of my jobs did. I felt like I was always working. I checked the time and realized I was supposed to have been off ten minutes ago. I needed to get over to the rental house and make sure it was cleaned up and ready for the client. My little rental property side gig was growing, which was great for the income, but it was also more stressful. The house was my latest acquisition. It was bigger and a little out of my way, but I was able to charge more. The vacation rental property thing was something I'd stumbled into. So far, it was working out. Except it was kicking my ass with all the running around. I couldn't afford to hire a cleaning company. I had to do it on my own. Along with the maintenance.

"Cindy, I need to go," I said to my manager.

"Five minutes," she said.

I rolled my eyes. "Fine, but then I have to go. I have a client checking in in an hour."

She slid over two cups. "To the big house?"

"Yep." I nodded. "My first client. The person that rented it says it's just one man."

"Ha!" she laughed. "You're going to have a bunch of frat boys in there."

"Don't say that," I groaned. "I purposely chose the house because it was off the beaten path. It doesn't invite the party type."

"Uh, maybe the fact it's off the beaten path is exactly why it's inviting," she said with a laugh.

"You better be wrong. I cannot afford to redo all the work I already did. That house put me in the red really fast."

"You made it beautiful," she said. "It's going to be a hot ticket once you get some reviews."

"I hope so," I said. "I'm going to go belly up if it fails. I put everything into buying that house."

"It's going to be fine," she said. "I'm just going to be sorry to lose you when you start making the big bucks. You'll be a real estate tycoon by next year."

"From your lips to God's ears," I scoffed.

"Did you finish the bathroom?" she asked as we worked alongside each other.

I nodded. "I did. It looks good if I do say so myself. Thank goodness for YouTube."

"You're going to be building your own house soon enough," she teased.

"Not a chance," I laughed. "I took a chance on a fixer upper. If it doesn't pay off, the only house I'm going to build is my straw hut. I will lose everything. I'm mortgaged to my eyeballs. I'm not sure if it was the right decision. I might have bitten off more than I can chew."

"It's going to be fine," she assured me. "Once you get a few reviews, you can up the rental price, and it will pay for itself. I'm sure of it."

"Thank you," I said with a sigh. "If not, I'm going to be looking for another job."

"How in the world do you plan on finding the time to take on another job?" she asked. "You have what, three?"

"And all of them combined still don't pay the bills," I replied.

I made decent money for a single woman. I would be doing just fine, better than fine if I didn't have a massive debt over my head. I felt stuck in the mud. I couldn't seem to move forward. The medical bills were ridiculous. I had argued and negotiated my father's medical bills as low as they were going to go. Now I was making huge monthly payments. I couldn't miss a payment. If I did, all my negotiating was for nothing. The money I made at the coffee shop was what I used to pay the medical bills. The money I made from my three rental properties was how I kept a roof over my head.

When my dad died, he was penniless. He'd been sick for a while. The insurance he had was pretty useless. He always tried to convince me to just let him go. He didn't want to be a burden. As if I could just give up on him. When he passed, it was devastating. Then came the cost of the funeral, and the medical bills seemed to keep coming in for months after he died. The burden nearly pulled me under. I refused to quit. I was determined to pay every penny. I was so close and yet so far. I was hoping the new rental house would push me over the top and I could finally move forward with my life.

I finished my shift and quickly rushed out to my car. I grabbed my purse and pulled out my makeup bag. I took a moment to freshen up after getting steam in my face the last few hours. I didn't think I was vain, but I wanted to present myself as a professional for the client I was going to be meeting. Assuming I met him. I was running late, which meant there was a good chance I might see him. I headed for the market to pick up a pineapple and a cheap bottle of wine.

The idea was to provide a nice welcome basket of sorts. The pineapple was a fun way to welcome the person to Hawaii. I did it with the condo I rented out. It was always mentioned in the reviews. The wine was extra because the house was extra. The guest was going to be my first review. It had to be good.

I checked the time and cringed. I was running late. I hoped he was as well. I rushed home to my small apartment in a not-so-great building. I would have lived in one of my own properties, but I could make more renting it out. I was keeping my eyes on the prize. There was a light at the end of the tunnel. I was hoping I would be able to pay off the medical bills in a year. Then it was full speed ahead and getting on with my own life.

Traffic was horrible as usual. Rain was adding to the chaos. Tourists were rushing around, trying to avoid the rain and not paying attention to traffic. The height of tourist season was over, but we always had tourists. I finally made it home and rushed into my ground floor apartment. Roxy, my Lab mix, hopped off the couch to greet me at the door.

"Hey, girl." I rubbed behind her ears while rushing toward the back door that opened to the very tiny yard I got to claim as my own. "You've got two minutes to do your business, then I have to go again."

I opened the door and let her out. She knew the drill. She ran in circles looking for the right spot. I pulled off the shirt splashed with coffee and whipped cream stains and tossed it in my dirty clothes basket. I rubbed on some deodorant and spritzed on my favorite fruity body spray. I hoped it would cover the scent of coffee that was sure to be clinging to me.

I stripped out of the black pants that were part of the uniform for the coffee shop. I wasn't trying to be fancy when I met the client. I wanted to be casual and welcoming. People came here for the Hawaii vibe of laid back. I refused to wear Hawaiian shirts. I pulled on a pair of jeans and scanned my closet for the right top. I went with the black top with shoulder cutouts. The black booties I wore all the time were by the door.

"Roxy!" I called out. "Come!"

I put on my shoes, ran my fingers through my thick, dark hair and called it good. Roxy's nails clacked across the vinyl floor as she rushed in. I refilled her water dish and tossed in a little kibble.

"I'll be back in an hour," I said. "Maybe two. You be a good girl. We'll go for a walk when I get back."

I rubbed her ears and kissed her nose. She was my best friend and the most loyal living thing I had ever met. I'd rescued her three years ago. She was a mutt but she was my mutt. I guessed she was a golden Lab mixed with I didn't know what, although she was smaller than a Lab. I was guessing maybe some hound dog, given her ears. She wasn't the prettiest dog on the planet, but she was mine.

I grabbed my purse and rushed right back out the door. It was the story of my life. I was always rushing to one place or another. I checked the time and winced again. "Dammit."

The house was about twenty minutes from my place. Thankfully, the rain was slowing. Unfortunately, that just meant the tourists were climbing out of their little hidey holes and clogging the streets once again. I turned right and hit the gas. My new rental property was away from the hustle and bustle of the tourist attractions. It was deep into the lush green of a hillside. I would have loved the house for myself, but not yet. When I bought the place, it had been in foreclosure and in rough shape. That was just over six months ago. I'd been busting ass getting it renovated and ready to be lived in. There was still more to be done on the place, but it was good enough for now. The property didn't look like much from the outside, but I had dumped money into the kitchen and master bathroom. A real estate investor told me to put my money there first.

I hoped he was right. If this thing blew up in my face, I was screwed. I might be able to sell it and break even, but then what? I hit the dirt road and slowed down. That was something I would have loved to be fixed, but it was a county road. The driveway to the house was much better. I just had to get my renters to the driveway without wanting to turn around and cancel their reservation.

"Please," I murmured.

I hoped my renter wasn't one of those that expected the Ritz while paying Motel Six prices.

Chapter Three

Ethan

"Fuck," I growled when I hit another pothole.

The listing said a dirt road. I was prepared for a solid dirt road, not the mud bog littered with potholes big enough to swallow the entire Porsche. I saw the driveway up ahead, relieved to find it was much smoother. The driveway was long, lined by natural foliage. I could feel my stress easing with every inch I got closer to the rental house.

When the house came into view, I stopped the car and looked at the place. There was a moment of regret. It was a little rough looking. I wondered if I'd been scammed. I'd paid a full month up front. The pictures on the Internet told a different story. It looked like the same house, but seeing it in person was different. It was new to the site and had no reviews.

I blew out a breath. I wasn't here for a luxurious vacation. I was hiding out. I really only needed a bed and a coffeemaker. I pulled the car to a stop in front of the garage. According to the homeowner, the garage door opener would be inside the house.

"Here goes nothing," I muttered.

I entered the code for the lock box on the front door and pulled out the key. My first impression when I walked in was fresh. I could smell fresh paint, and it was very clean. Despite the gray clouds outside, it was bright with all the windows. The open floor plan made it feel much bigger than it was. I barely paid attention to the kitchen and the sleek black appliances against the white cabinets. The stairs were in front of me. I wasn't going to sleep in a shithole. If the bed looked sketchy, I was out. The listing boasted five bedrooms, but I was guessing the bedrooms were the size of closets.

I carried the suitcase up the stairs and paused at the landing. There was a single door on the left and several down the hall to the right. I was going to assume the master was on the left. I pushed open the door and took it in for a moment. It wasn't huge or luxurious, but it looked and smelled clean. I left my suitcase by the door and tossed the garment bag on the bed. I pushed back the sheer curtains and took in the view of nothing but green. The backyard looked like a tidy jungle. There was a large pond that apparently had koi fish. It was shaped like a comma, surrounded by more of the green foliage with bright red flowers on the top.

It was exactly what I needed. I could see rooftops of other houses, but that was it. In the distance, I could see blue and knew it was the ocean. It was nearly a mile away, but I knew it was there. The silence welcomed me. The solitude wrapped around me, blocking out all things New York. I closed my eyes and took a deep breath. It felt like the first deep breath I had taken in days.

"Hello?"

My eyes popped open, and my anger skyrocketed. *What the fuck?* The owner of the house had promised I would be alone. It was a no-contact entry. I'd paid for privacy. I didn't want anyone bugging me, and the owner had assured me there wouldn't be. Pissed, I spun on my heel and jogged downstairs, ready to lay into the woman in my house.

I stopped short when I saw an attractive woman in the kitchen. She was arranging a pineapple and bottle of wine in a basket. I didn't get it. "Can I help you?" I asked irritably.

She whipped her head around, and I got my first real look at her. She was very pretty. Dark chestnut hair hung down her back and shoulders. Her eyes were just as dark as her hair. She wasn't a native Hawaiian. I didn't think. She smiled at me, revealing perfect teeth. "Hi," she said with a small wave.

She stepped forward and extended her hand. I took it out of habit. "Hello."

"I'm Ava Hunt," she said with the same bright smile. She was perky. Too perky. I wasn't in the mood for happiness and joy. I wanted to sulk. I assumed she was a neighbor or maybe the housekeeper.

"Ethan Mitchell," I said in a hard voice. I was about to tell her to leave when she cut me off.

"I wanted to be here to greet you," she said. "I got caught up at work."

"Who are you?" I asked.

"I'm Ava Hunt," she said with a confused frown. "I own the house."

That confused me. She didn't look like someone who owned a property like this. "You're the property owner?"

"I am. Did you just get in?"

"Yes." I nodded. I looked on the small, square island in the kitchen. "Is that a pineapple?"

"Yes!" She smiled brightly. "It's just something I like to do for my guests. There's a handy gadget in the drawer that will cut it. I hand-picked it. The wine and cheese is just my little way of saying thank you for taking a chance on a new rental with no reviews."

She was talking fast. And way too excitedly for my current mood. "Thanks."

"I'll show you around and then get out of your hair," she said.

"I think I can find my way around," I said. "It's not that big of a house."

She smirked and didn't seem to take offense to my comment. "No, I guess it's not."

"I've already put my things upstairs," I told her.

"In the master?"

"I would assume it was the master." I shrugged.

"There are two other bedrooms upstairs," she said. "You have the master bath, which has been completely remodeled." She started to walk, and I found myself following her like a damn puppy. "This is the half bath." She opened a door. "Down here is a guest bedroom with a full bath."

"Is there a basement?" I asked.

"No."

"I thought there were five bedrooms," I questioned.

"Ah, there is a guest house." She smiled. "Although it isn't really ready. I thought you booked the place for just yourself."

"I did," I replied. "I was just wondering."

"I can show you out there," she said.

"No!" I realized it had come out a little loudly. "I don't plan on using it. I don't need to see it."

"Oka." She nodded and walked to the French doors that led to the large deck that wrapped around the house. "The propane grill is new and ready to use. You'll find tools in the kitchen."

I looked at the grill and tried to remember the last time I had ever used one. Probably in college. I wasn't sure that was a good thing. I wouldn't even know how to.

"If you'd like to feed the koi, please only do it once a day," she said. "Their food is in that small shed." She pointed across the lush lawn that didn't actually look like the manicured grass at my house. It was more of a natural landscape. "There is an automatic feeder that ensures they are fed if you don't want to do it."

"Got it," I said.

"While you're pretty secluded out here, I always ask people to lock the doors," she said. "Please make sure the stove is off before you leave the house. Trust me, I have to say it because it has happened before. The driveway is usually fine, but you might have noticed the road can get a little rough when it rains. The garage door opener is on the table. All the appliances are new, so I don't anticipate any issues. There are dishes and everything else you'll need for your stay."

I was nodding but not paying attention. I wasn't twelve. I knew how to live on my own. "Got it."

"And guests are fine, even overnight once but please remember, this is a home," she said. "No parties. A couple friends over is fine, but I've put a lot of blood, sweat, and tears into this place. Your neighbors might not hear anything, but it's still not okay. Also, no swimming in the pond. It's really not sanitary."

I wondered what kind of people she'd been renting to that made her feel like she needed to say all of this. Wasn't it kind of understood? Who in the hell would go swimming in a koi pond? "Anything else?" I asked irritably. "I'd like to unpack."

She frowned and tapped her finger on the rail of the deck. "Just know you are responsible for your own daily cleaning. I can come in once a week to do a deep clean and change the bedding and stuff. It's something I offer my premium guests."

"Premium guests?" I asked.

"Yes." She smiled. "You are a premium guest."

"Good to know," I muttered.

"Okay, well, here's my card," she said and handed me a business card. "The remote and a channel guide are in the kitchen in the drawer labeled guides and things."

"Thanks," I said.

"Okay, well, enjoy your pineapple!"

I followed her back into the house and watched her leave. She was not what I'd expected as the property owner. I had met plenty of realtors in my life. They were either slick salesmen or women that wore way too much makeup and had big hair and short skirts. This lady, Ava, looked normal. Obviously beautiful but normal. After making sure she left the property, I went back upstairs to unpack.

I carried my toiletry bag into the bathroom and was actually impressed. It was nice. I unpacked my stuff and went back into the bedroom to hang the garment bag. The house wasn't like anything I had stayed in before. I had been born with a silver spoon in my mouth. I'd grown up in a mansion and had my own now. When I traveled, I stayed in penthouses. I didn't cook for myself. I only did the very basic cleanup duties at home. I had two assistants that handled my schedule and basically ran my life. And it was a busy life. I was constantly on the go. Everyone wanted a piece of me. It had been that way for my whole life. As the firstborn, it was understood that I would one day take over the company. That had been decided before I had even been born. It was a lot of pressure.

I had taken the pressure in stride, but it was suddenly too much. I felt the walls closing in on me. Then my fucking brother and his bullshit. As head of the company and the family, everything my brother did blew back on me. I had kept my nose clean. No scandals. But now I was dealing with his bullshit.

Or not dealing with it. That's why I was in Hawaii. I had to get my head straight before I did something drastic. I was feeling pushed into a corner. I was ready to tear up my birth certificate, grab a little cash, and hop on a plane to anywhere and never look back. Hawaii was my escape. It was a test to see if I could really walk away.

Chapter Four

Ava

The guy was an asshole. He was handsome, and if I had to guess, wealthy. He had that look about him. I knew the type. I had been raised with them. Rich men had a certain look, and Ethan had it. He looked like a man that was used to the finer things in life. The Porsche in the driveway said it all. I had to laugh at the idea of a Porsche navigating the shitty road. If that didn't scream rich and spoiled, I didn't know what did.

It was too bad he was a dick. He was very attractive. I always had a thing for the guys with a sharp edge. I didn't know why, considering it always blew up in my face. Edgy guys usually had baggage. That baggage always got in the way of a relationship. I was tired of shitty relationships and had just decided not to date again.

I liked to think I was the kind of person that could judge people pretty well. Not really judge, but I could size them up. When people came into the coffee shop, I could immediately gauge their moods. Ethan was a man with a heavy burden. There was a darkness behind the light hazel eyes. His dark hair was longer than the usual clean business type I remembered from my days in New York. It was messy, like he'd been running his hands through it, which made me think he was stressed. Then there was the five o'clock shadow. It was new, which said he normally shaved. I knew from his rental info he was from New York. I was guessing he was a Wall Street guy or some hotshot in the corporate world. I didn't follow the market, but maybe he'd lost some money. Lost his job. Lost a wife. His shitty mood was likely because of one of those things.

I wasn't going to let it bother me. A little time on our beautiful island might snap him out of the funk he was in. It wasn't like I had to be friends with him. My goal was to make sure he had a good stay. Good enough for him to leave me a good review. Happiness was a choice. That was something I learned from a woman I did chores for as one of my many side jobs. It had been shortly after my father died. I had that same look I saw in Ethan's eyes. It was the look of someone just wanting to give up. I remembered wanting to roll over and just let life kick me around.

Then I was told it was my choice. I could give up, or I could choose to be happy and push on. My old friend had passed away, but her advice resonated deep within. Every day I had to decide to be happy. I wasn't a Pollyanna by any means. I had my moments. I bawled on occasion. I got mad sometimes. Ethan was not the kind of guy that was going to appreciate my cheesy advice, and I wouldn't presume to give it.

I stopped by the grocery store and picked up a few things before heading home. It was one of my slower days. I was looking forward to a cold beer, nachos, and whatever I could find on Netflix. Although I had put in a full eight hour day between all my jobs, it felt like a day off.

"Roxy!" I called out her name while kicking the door shut behind me.

She didn't immediately come running to me, which meant I had interrupted her nap. I heard her slow walk into the kitchen while I put away the groceries. She yawned, stretched, and then gave a good shake.

"Did I wake you?" I asked.

She yawned again and looked at the last bag on the counter. She knew it was her treats. "One treat," I said. "Do you need to go potty?"

Her gaze was focused on the bag. I opened up the package of treats and gave her one. She rushed to the spot on the rug in the living room where she always took her treats. It didn't matter if she was lying on the couch or asleep in her bed in my room. Treats had to be consumed in that one spot. While she busied herself, I grabbed a cold beer, opened it, and leaned against the counter to search my email.

I was hoping to have another reservation for the house. Unfortunately, there was nothing. The mortgage payment was coming up. I'd hoped to have a couple more reservations to pay for the mortgage on the damn thing. It had to happen, or I was going to be in deep shit.

Roxy came into the kitchen with her tail wagging. "Ready to go outside?" I asked her.

She yipped in response. With beer in hand, I walked out back with her. I sat down in one of the two chairs and watched her run around. I could hear my neighbors' kids on the other side of the fence. I was lucky to have good neighbors. On one side was a young married couple with a couple of kids. My other neighbors were a middle-aged couple. I was surrounded by happily married people. It made my own single status very real at times.

I listened to the kids and their parents. It wasn't that I wanted to be single. I did crave a partner, but I just couldn't find the right one. The few guys I had dated in the last year had proven to be untrustworthy and basically pieces of shit in general. The one boyfriend I'd had turned out to be a piece of shit as well. I didn't trust easily, and after a string of bad dates, I was done trying. I had been told more times than I could count that I would find the right guy eventually. When we met, I would just know he was the one. I was hoping there would be a bight neon arrow pointing at the guy that made it perfectly clear I was on the right path. I didn't want to take chances stumbling onto the wrong one.

Roxy meandered over, letting me know she was ready to go back inside. I flopped onto the couch with her immediately climbing up to sit next to me. I rubbed her neck and stared at the picture on the wall to my right. I loved the picture. I talked to the picture of my father more than I cared to admit. It was from one of the last really good days I'd had with him before lung cancer made it almost impossible to do much of anything.

I smiled at the memory of that day.

"Ava! Look! Do you see them?" He pointed in the direction of splashing water.

I pushed up my sunglasses and studied the water. "Ah!" I shouted. "I see them! Will they get closer?"

"If you stop screaming at them, they might," Richard, one of my father's closest friends, laughed.

I had to remind myself not to jump up and down in the boat. I didn't want to fall over the side. Although if a dolphin rescued me, it wouldn't be the worst thing in the world. I was loving life. I'd come to Hawaii to visit my father, but I didn't think I was ever going to leave. It was beautiful and best of all, it was far from New York and my manipulative family.

"Watch, Ava," Dad said again with his hand on my shoulder. "Here they come."

My dad and I and his two old Navy buddies stayed perfectly still while the dolphins swam closer. When they got close, I took a couple of pictures. My dad stepped forward. He turned to look at me, grinning big while leaning to the side. I snapped a picture of him just as a dolphin jumped out of the water.

I snapped out of the memory. That week had been amazing. It was what had changed my mind. I went home, packed my shit, and moved to Hawaii to stay. It sucked because I had only been with my dad a couple of months when we learned he was sick. He fought for two long years. His friends had become my honorary uncles. Between all of us, we supported and looked after him. When Dad died, I would never forget how they circled the wagons around me.

The VA had not covered a lot of the extra stuff that was needed to keep him comfortable in the last months. Those were the bills that I was still paying for. My credit cards and his had been maxed just trying to cover living expenses. The VA covered as little as possible. I refused to let my dad be treated poorly. I put myself into debt making sure he had the best of the best in those final months. I didn't regret it for a minute, even when I was running on four hours of sleep because I was working three jobs.

My only regret was not getting to spend more time with my dad. I was still very bitter about the situation. My dad had been stationed in Hawaii during his last years in the Navy. I had been young and didn't understand how lucky we were to get to live on a beautiful island. I never did learn the specifics about why, but one day, Mom packed our things, and we got on a plane to New York. We never turned back. New York had been a different world. My mother's wealthy family was nothing like the people we had associated with in Hawaii. It took a long time for me to get my bearings.

It wasn't until after I graduated college that I finally took the initiative to visit my dad in Hawaii. My eyes went back to the picture. I'd missed out on a lifetime with my dad, and it still pissed me off. I would never forgive my mother and her family for keeping me from my father. I supposed there was a backstory, but I was certain it was about my father's career. His lack of money. His desire to live a low-key life did not match their New York blue-blood lifestyle.

"Oh Roxy," I sighed and rubbed her ear. "People suck."

She didn't budge. She was used to me talking to her all the time. She was really my only friend. The only one I could trust. The humans had not proven themselves to even be half as trustworthy as dogs. I'd gotten Roxy after my dad died. Richard had insisted I get a dog. He took me to the shelter and was there to help me pick just the right one. But like many people always said, Roxy chose me.

"Huh, girl?" I said and bent down to kiss her soft fur. "You picked me. You hopped up from your bed and came right to me."

It had been love at first sight. And Richard had been right: Roxy saw me through some rough nights. "Are you hungry?" I asked her.

I could sit and mull over my late father and all the reasons I was pissed off that I didn't get the chance to know him better, or pull up my big girl panties and make some dinner.

I hopped up and fried some hamburger for my nachos. After feeding Roxy, I sat on the couch and settled in for the night. I thought about texting Ethan to make sure everything was okay, but I didn't think he would appreciate me bugging him. I always texted my renters to make sure they had everything they needed. It was another perk. Sometimes they said yes. Sometimes they asked about this or that. But Ethan was not the kind of guest that wanted me to ask him if he'd found the corkscrew. If he needed something, he would reach out to me.

Chapter Five

Ethan

I tied my shoe and jumped to my feet. It was nice and early. I would have preferred to sleep in, but sleep had eluded me. Despite being sleep deprived, I felt better than I had in a long time. I couldn't wait to get down to the beach. I left my phone on the table. That was unheard of for me. It was like leaving my arm behind. But it felt good. I walked down the driveway and then started to jog toward the beach.

There were a few beachcombers but not many. Thankfully, the house was in an area with no hotels. I imagined most of the houses were second homes. I jogged along the beach, inhaling the sea air. Birds squawked and screeched overhead. The sounds and smells took me back to one of the times I had been in Hawaii. It was the trip after I'd graduated and just a few weeks before I headed off to bootcamp.

Those were the good days. I wasn't the CEO. My only concern was finding the next party and looking for a woman to hook up with. My friends and I all came from money. We didn't have to worry about partying late and getting up for work the next morning. We didn't have to worry about blowing too much money. Life had been so easy back then.

If I went back in time, I could pinpoint the very day my life started to go to hell. It was the day I put on the suit and walked into the office as CEO of the company. It had been like stepping into a pair of cement shoes, and they had only gotten heavier over the years.

After running thirty minutes, I turned back and jogged to the house. It was a little strange to be walking. I was a little too used to my gilded cage. It was strange, but I felt free. I felt like I had escaped my cage and was on the lam. It was kind of exciting. I couldn't remember the last time I had felt youthful and free. This was my grand adventure. How long it lasted was yet to be determined. If things went well, maybe forever.

I made it back to the house and immediately went for the shower. I was glad my landlord had decided to put some money into the bathroom. There were few things in life that could beat a good shower. I was feeling good, thinking about what I was going to do with all my free time. I wanted to go sailing. I had not gone sailing in forever. In high school, I had been on the sailing team. I remembered the freedom of being on the open water with the wind blowing through my hair and the feel of the spray on my face.

I stepped out of the shower with my mind made up. I was going to rent a boat for the day. I slung a towel around my hips and brushed my teeth. I rubbed my hand over my jaw and thought about shaving. It was part of the routine. Part of my corporate look. But that was my life in New York. The life I was trying to leave behind. I put back the razor and dried my face.

It was nice to not think about what suit I was going to wear. I pulled on a pair of cargo shorts and a T-shirt. There wasn't much in the way of food in the house, but there was coffee. I doubted I was going to be able to get delivery, which meant I was going to have to travel back over that shitty road in search of sustenance.

I had committed to ignoring my phone and email when I hopped on the plane yesterday. So far, I had stuck to that. Unfortunately, I couldn't actually run away. I did have hundreds of people counting on me. They'd done nothing wrong. Their only mistake was working for our company. I had to think about them and their futures.

I put my phone on speaker and called my personal voicemail. As expected, it was full. I imagined there were a lot of people looking for me. While the messages played, I looked at the K-cup selections.

"Ethan!"

I jumped when I heard my mother's voice. It was like I was ten, and she'd walked into the kitchen to catch me with my hand in the cookie jar.

"Where are you? Ethan, this isn't funny. You have to call me back. Did you get Collin's message? You have to talk to us, Ethan. I am really hoping you're just playing a stupid game and aren't actually hurt. For all I know, you might be lying in a ditch bleeding out. Call me."

I pushed the button to delete the message. My mother had the dramatics down. She could win an Oscar.

"Ethan, it's me." I heard my brother's voice. "Dude, you have to call me. I'm spinning out here. Shit is about to hit the fan. I need you. You have to help me. I don't know where you are, but Mom and Dad are losing their shit. I'm going out to the Hampton house. I hope you're there. This is not the time to play hide and seek. Call me back. Bye."

I rolled my eyes and shook my head. Collin was in trouble. Surprise. He was always in trouble. The guy took full advantage of his spare status. I was the heir, he was the spare. No one ever expected anything of him. He got to choose his own path. He ran around doing what he wanted. Unfortunately, it wasn't always within the legal boundaries. He liked to push the envelope. He knew his name and our father's money would get him out of any trouble. Not just get him out of the trouble but bury anything that would negatively impact his reputation. Collin had political aspirations and needed to keep his nose clean. Except he didn't. He was thirty-two and acted like a frat boy.

"Ethan." My father's deep, commanding voice echoed around the kitchen.

I cringed and stopped what I was doing. That was the kind of effect he had on me. I was a grown-ass man, and he could still whip me into shape with a single word.

"This is beneath you," he said sternly. "As the CEO of a billion-dollar company, you have certain responsibilities. Those cannot be shirked because someone said something that hurt your feelings. This is the real world. Mitchells don't run. We stick together. I'm not sure where you are, but I'm not in the mood for games. I'm not interested in hide and seek. You're an adult. Get your ass to the house and handle this like a grownup. We have to get ahead of this. You are a member of the family, and I expect you to behave like one. I'll expect to see you within the hour."

I deleted the message and exited the voicemail. I didn't want to hear anything else. I wasn't surprised. They had figured out I flew the coop. I wasn't surprised. I couldn't help but smile at the fact that I had managed to escape without anyone knowing where I was. My plan had worked. For now, at least. My dad would send out a search party. He would find me. What happened once he did find me was hard to say. I was a little big to be dragged home by my collar.

Collin had screwed up. Not me. Why was I the one to clean up the mess he made? I couldn't even count how many messes I had cleaned up. I did it to protect the company and the family. They were intertwined. If the family name was tarnished, the company would suffer. I did all the clean-up work. Always. As if I didn't have enough on my plate. I was running the company. I had more than enough on my plate. Why did they think I should have to deal with Collin's bullshit? I didn't know the specifics of his latest scandal, and I didn't want to know. It sounded bad, like the kind of thing that landed people in prison. I wanted nothing to do with it. He needed a lawyer—not me.

My phone rang just as I took the first sip of coffee. I glanced down and saw my mother's number. I didn't want to answer. But if I didn't, she'd keep calling. There was also the chance there was actually something wrong. More wrong than my brother fucking around with the wrong woman. I loved my family even though we weren't quite a Hallmark family. We had love for one another, but we weren't the touch-feely type. We stuck together, but it felt like it was more of a necessity than a desire. We had to protect the family name. At all costs.

"Hello," I answered.

"Ethan!" Her exclamation was her usual over-dramatization. "Oh goodness! You're alive! I was so worried. You can't do that to me."

"I'm fine, Mom," I said.

"Where are you?"

"I'm on vacation," I answered.

"Collin went to the Hampton house, and he said you weren't there and had not been there," she said.

"Because I'm not there," I replied.

"Where are you?"

"What do you need, Mom?" I asked.

"Are you honestly not going to tell me where you are?" she asked with irritation.

"No, I'm not," I said. "What do you need?"

"I need my son here to help us through this," she said and switched back to crying. "Ethan, it just seems to get worse every day. This is bad. This is going to take him down. It could take all of us down."

"Mom, there is nothing I can do," I said. "Let the lawyers handle it. Neither you nor Dad should be getting involved. If it turns out Collin is involved, there are going to be legal ramifications. Serious consequences, Mom."

"Which is why you need to be here," she moaned. "We've consulted with Jordan. He told us to lay low and wait to see what happens. He isn't a criminal defense attorney and said he would refer us to a colleague. Criminal defense, Ethan! Can you imagine?"

I sighed. "Mom, it's better to get a lawyer now. If Collin is innocent, it will come out. I can't do anything. He screwed up. We have always told him that one of these days, it was going to catch up with him."

"Stop it!" she scolded. "This isn't a joke. He could be in serious trouble."

"Someone died, Mom! He should be in trouble!"

"Don't you dare tell me you believe your brother had anything to do with that," she gasped.

"I don't believe anything because we don't have the facts," I said. "I'm not interested in getting involved."

"You are involved," she sobbed. "You're family."

"I don't know what he did or didn't do," I said. "I don't want to know. I want to maintain plausible deniability. I think you might want to as well. We don't know where this thing is going. You don't want to get stuck testifying against him."

"Don't say that!" I heard her audibly sobbing and blowing her nose. "I don't know how we'll get through this. It will destroy us. What about the company? I can't deal with this. I won't be able to show my face. Your father and I will have to move. I don't know what you're going to do about the company. You have to prepare yourself and the company. We stand to lose everything. This is serious."

I knew it was serious. I knew we stood to lose a lot. All because my brother couldn't grow the hell up. He was single-handedly going to take down an empire that had been around for generations. It was too much to get my head around. I kept thinking about everything I had sacrificed to keep the family business going. I didn't get to play and party. I didn't get to pursue a career in the Air Force because I had to go back and learn the ropes to take over the company. I gave up so much to keep the family business going.

"I have to go," I said.

"Ethan—"

I ended the call. I was so done. My parents were going to continue to cater to my younger brother. He was the way he was because no one told him to stop. He was never held accountable. Now, we were all going to pay the price.

Chapter Six

Ava

The poodle pulled on the leash, causing me to trip. I barely managed to catch myself. "King, slow down," I ordered.

The other three smaller dogs I was walking were trying to keep up with the poodle, who thought he really was king of the world. I held the three leashes attached to the smaller dogs in one hand and King's leash in my other hand.

"Stop," I called out when we came to the corner of the street.

We waited for the road to clear and quickly crossed. Walking dogs wasn't necessarily hard. It was about choreography. I scheduled my clients based on the size of their dogs. I had made the mistake of trying to walk three large dogs at once and nearly died. They'd walked me. I was the dummy trying to hold on to the leashes.

Out of nowhere, a bird flew down and landed on the sidewalk a few feet in front of the dogs. "Shit," I muttered and pulled back on the leashes. "King, don't you do it!"

It was too late. He started barking, which triggered the other dogs. They were all barking. "Shoo, bird! Shoo!"

In the midst of the barking, I heard my phone ringing. "Perfect timing," I murmured.

I quickly pulled my phone out and saw it was the renter. I couldn't afford to miss his call. I switched all the leashes to one hand. "Hello," I answered cheerily.

The dogs were pulling and barking at the stupid bird that was leisurely eating food that had been dropped. "Hello?" I heard Ethan say.

"Yes?"

"This is Ethan Mitchell," he said.

"Yes, Mr. Mitchell," I said and pulled back on the leashes again. "Did you need something? Is everything okay?"

"Actually, no," he said. "What is that noise? Can you hear me?"

Thankfully, the bird flew away. The dogs tried to chase it. "I can hear you," I answered.

The dogs started to quiet down. I pulled the leashes to get them back on the sidewalk and on our usual route.

"I seem to be lost," he said. "Lost and stuck."

"Where are you?"

"If I knew, I wouldn't be lost," he growled.

I laughed at the irony. "Good point. Okay, do you see any signs? Houses?"

"No. Nothing. My GPS isn't working out here. It was and then it wasn't. I thought I had the route down and exited off the map. Now I'm stuck. Literally."

"Stuck?" I asked. I could hear his frustration. I knew he was irritated, but I had to ask the questions if I was going to help him. And I assumed he wanted my help because he was calling.

"Yes, stuck! The car is stuck in mud that is practically knee high. I tried to call a tow truck, but they can't pull the car out if they don't know where it is. I can't tell them where it is because I don't know."

"I understand," I said calmly. "Can you tell me where you were? Were you leaving the house or going somewhere else?"

"I went to get groceries," he said. "I was on my way back."

"What store?"

He gave me a rundown of where he had been, which helped me get a general idea of where he might be. "Did you say you didn't have service?" I asked, only then realizing he was calling me.

"I don't have service where the car is stuck," he said with a sigh. "I walked until I did. But it's not like there are road signs. There's nothing."

I was already walking the dogs back to their homes. "I'll head out there."

"Do you know where you are going?" he asked dryly.

"I have a general idea," I replied.

"Fine," he sighed. "I'll be sitting here. In the mud."

"Did you get your groceries?" I asked.

"I did."

"Grab a snack and get comfortable," I told him.

I sped up and quickly dropped the dogs off before walking to my own car. I was pretty sure I knew where he was. There was a road about half a mile before the house that led up into the mountains. It was horrible, and most people rode bikes up the hill. It was rough even in a Jeep. I couldn't imagine taking a sports car up there.

I turned off the road and very slowly navigated around the holes while avoiding the edges where the mud was thick. It didn't take long for me to find him. I was surprised to find he had made it as far as he did. He was leaning against the back of the car with a bag of chips in his hand. He looked very casual in his shorts and T-shirt. Almost too casual. His hair was mussed, which was the look he was going for, I surmised. It was hot. I could almost imagine him being the star of some kind of commercial for the chips. The car was tilted to the right with the passenger side wheels sank into the mud. I stopped my car and got out with a smile on my face.

"Hi," I said.

"Hello."

He made no move to pull away from the car. "I'm here," I said.

"I see that."

"I don't have service right here," I told him. "It's a dead spot. We can call a tow truck from the road."

"How long do you think it will take for them to get here?" he asked.

"I don't know, thirty minutes," I shrugged. "I know a guy."

"You know a guy?" he scoffed.

"Yes." I smiled. "He owns a tow company. I'll call him and ask him to come out sooner rather than later. With the recent rains, I imagine the tow companies are going to be busy pulling other tourists from the mud."

"I'm not a tourist," he shot back.

I smirked. "But you are."

"Whatever. Fine. Call."

"Why don't we put your groceries in my car," I said like I was talking to a child in the midst of a tantrum. "We'll call and then take your stuff to the house while we wait for the tow truck."

"I can't have some yahoo pulling this car out of the mud," he complained. "This is not my car. I'm renting it. These cars shouldn't be jerked around."

"Trust me, you are not the first hot shot to get an expensive sports car stuck in the mud or the sand," I said. "If you'd like to call someone else, be my guest."

He wiped his hand on his shorts and pulled open the door. I assumed that meant he was getting his stuff. He reached out with a bag in his hand, indicating he wanted me to take it. After putting the three bags of groceries in my car, I got in and waited for him to get into the passenger seat. He opened the door and paused.

"Oops," I said and grabbed the lint brush I kept in the console. I quickly ran it over the front seat where Roxy's hair had been clinging.

He sat down like he was sitting in a pile of shit. It would have been offensive if it wasn't so funny. "Ready?" I asked.

"As I'll ever be," he muttered.

"Sorry about the dog hair," I said and carefully turned around to point the car back down the hill. "Roxy always rides shotgun."

"Roxy?"

"My dog," I answered with a laugh.

"I see."

As soon as we got service, I called my friend. He promised to be out within the hour. "Should we go put your groceries away?" I asked. "I would hate for your beer to get warm."

"I don't plan on drinking it for breakfast," he replied.

He was surly. I wasn't sure if he was pissed at me or just pissed in general. "Were you doing some sightseeing?" I asked conversationally.

"No. I was going to get food."

"Have you had breakfast?" I asked.

"No," he replied grumpily. "I was going to make breakfast."

"I haven't eaten yet either," I said. "I know a great place not too far away. We could get breakfast together."

"No thanks," he muttered.

"I think you must have low blood sugar or something," I said. "You're cranky."

"I'm not cranky."

"You're in the most beautiful place in the world, and you're in a bad mood," I said. "You can choose to be happy, or you can choose to be pissed off in what some people refer to as Eden."

He scoffed. "I'm not in a bad mood."

"I know how to help you be happy," I said, not letting his crappy attitude bring me down. If I didn't turn his mood around, he was likely going to leave me a shitty review. I needed to make him happier.

"What would that be?" he asked.

"The best pancakes you will ever eat," I said with a bright smile. "We'll take your groceries in and make sure the tow truck finds the car. I'll have him drop it off at the house. You'll get recharged with a delicious breakfast. I'll bring you back here, and the day will be yours to do with as you please."

He let out a long sigh. "Fine."

I didn't mean to laugh, but it came out anyway. "All right, that sounds like an excited yes."

I pulled up the driveway and parked the car. We carried the bags into the kitchen. I noticed the pineapple, wine and cheese were still on the counter. I didn't say anything. I casually put the pineapple in the fridge along with the cheese. I realized the wine was probably a little too cheap for his tastes. He was likely used to the best of the best. I didn't care. It was the thought that counted.

"Ready?" I asked him after we put things away.

"As I'll ever be."

He was still acting like a pouty child. I wasn't going to let it bother me. If he was still in an asshole mood, that was on him. I could only do so much. I wasn't sure what had brought him to Oahu by himself, but whatever it was, it was clearly hanging over him. He sat quietly in the passenger seat, staring out the window. I was guessing it was girl trouble. He probably had an ex back home that had either cheated on him or he'd cheated on her and was hiding out. Or maybe he'd lost all his money. He didn't have sadness in his eyes, so I didn't think it was a death he was trying to run from. I knew sadness. I knew the look. He was angry. So much anger.

I saw the tow truck and followed him up the road. He jumped out and put his hands on his hips and stared at the car. Ethan and I got out and stood beside the driver. "These cars don't belong on backroads," he said.

I felt Ethan's anger. I cleared my throat and stepped forward. "Can you get it out without damaging it?" I asked.

"Sure, just needs a little tug. I can call for a flatbed if you don't want to take it down the road."

"No," Ethan answered. "Just get it out of the mud. I'll take it down. I made it up."

In a few minutes, it was out of the mud. Ethan paid in cash, and we were off. I followed him back to the house, and to my surprise, he got back into my car without saying a word. "Ready?" I asked with a bright smile.

"I've got the distinct feeling I don't really have a choice," he muttered.

"Of course, you have a choice," I answered. "You have the choice to eat an amazing breakfast or not."

"Are you one of those people that is into yoga and nature and all that?" he asked.

"I like yoga. I do love nature. I'm not sure what *all that* is, but I have learned being angry takes a lot more energy than just being at peace."

He made another snorting sound. I really hoped I could show him a little joy. I didn't know the man, but I hated that he was in such a state. No one deserved to feel like that.

Chapter Seven

Ethan

I didn't understand why she was so invested in me being happy. She didn't know me. I would never see her again after I left. It was strange. I wasn't used to anyone being so worried about my happiness. People were usually concerned if I was pissed only if they were worried they were going to get fired. I glanced over at Ava. There was a peacefulness about her. I wondered what that was like. I couldn't remember ever feeling that. I was definitely a Type A personality. When I did something, I gave it my all. I didn't stop until it was perfect.

She pulled into a gravel parking lot somewhere way out of the way. There were actual chickens scratching in the gravel. My first thought was to stay in the car. "This is a restaurant?" I asked.

"It is." She grinned. "It's top secret. The outside is designed to scare away the tourists. We like to keep some things just for us."

"I don't think there are going to be a lot of people clamoring to get in here," I said dryly.

"Exactly! That means they will have a table for us. We won't have to wait."

"Are you pulling my leg, or is this an actual restaurant?" I asked.

She laughed again and shut off the car. "It's an actual restaurant."

I pointed to the chickens. "Am I looking at the menu?"

"No." She laughed again. "But they are responsible for the fresh eggs that will be served with your breakfast."

I shook my head and climbed out of the car. "This is the weirdest thing I've ever seen. It's like we're in a third world country."

"You sound very judgmental," she chided.

I didn't think it was all that judge-y to be a little concerned about eating at a restaurant with chickens roaming around out front. She pulled open the door and gestured for me to go inside. I stepped in and immediately scanned the area. It was a small place, maybe ten tables tops. A few people were eating. A very large man peered at us through the pass-through. He was definitely a local.

"Ava!"

An older woman with dark skin and white hair met us at the door. "Hi, Makana," Ava said and gave the woman a hug.

"Who's your friend?" Makana asked with a bright smile.

"Makana, this is Ethan," she said. "I promised to treat him to the best breakfast on the whole island."

Makana looked me up and down. "You need it," she said.

I wasn't sure that was her being nice. "Thanks," I said.

"Go sit down," Makana said. "I'll bring you some juice."

I followed Ava to a table and took a seat. There was a single menu on the table. I picked it up, but Ava pulled it from my hand. "What's wrong?" I asked.

"You want the macadamia nut pancakes," she said. "Hashbrowns and the best, freshest bacon you'll ever eat. And of course, the eggs. How do you like them?"

"Are you sure you don't want to tell me?" I asked sarcastically.

"If I were you, I'd go over easy." She shrugged. "That's what I'm going with."

Makana rushed over and delivered two glasses of orange juice. "Do you know what you want?" she asked.

"Apparently, Ava knows what I want," I answered.

Makana frowned at me. I got the impression she didn't like me. Ava smiled and quickly gave our order. I sipped the juice, impressed by the sweetness. It tasted fresh.

"What was that noise when I called you earlier?" I asked curiously.

"Dogs," she answered.

"You have more than one?"

"No, I have just the one," she replied. "I was walking four other dogs."

"Why?"

"Because it's my job," she said.

"You're a dog walker?" I asked with surprise.

She nodded. "I am."

"Are you the property manager or is it your property?" I asked. I felt like I was interrogating her, but I had so many questions. She intrigued me.

"It's my property," she said. "I have the house, a condo, and a small apartment."

"Wow," I said. "Why do you walk the dogs then?"

"If that surprises you, I'll really blow your mind when I tell you I also work morning shifts at a local coffee shop," she said with a laugh. She looked embarrassed. She was laughing it off, but I was picking up on the embarrassment.

"Is it the cost of living here?" I asked. "I've read it's pretty steep. I know property is expensive."

She shrugged and looked away. "It is high. A lot of people work several jobs. I know that's probably hard for you to understand, but it's necessary for many. I don't expect you to know what it's like not to be able to afford to pay rent."

"You're right." I nodded. "I've been fortunate. I don't have to worry about things like that. However, I do admire you and anyone else that works that hard. Hard work is something I respect. It says a lot about a person willing to put in the effort to keep a roof over their heads. I respect that."

"Oh." She blinked. Clearly, she had not been expecting me to agree with her.

"You're surprised," I said.

"I don't know if I'm surprised, but it's nice to hear someone like you acknowledge that people who don't have a lot aren't lazy. They work just as hard, maybe harder than people that have been lucky enough to be born into the right family or are crazy smart and can invent something."

"I absolutely acknowledge it," I said. "I know I've been lucky. I don't think there is enough understanding between people. People judge and assume without really knowing someone's story."

She gave me a curious look. "That's very—"

I raised an eyebrow. "Very—?"

"Insightful," she said. "I agree. People are too worried about what other people think. One person's standards are not another's. What makes one person happy does not always make another person happy. I just wish we could all take a step back and let people live the way they want."

She had her own secrets. There was a story behind her words. I was interested to learn more. But that would have to wait. Plates piled high with food were delivered. I stared at the spread with big eyes. Ava was looking at me with a bright grin.

"Prepare to be wowed," she said.

I watched her pour syrup over her stack of pancakes before she handed it to me. I followed her lead and poured some over my pancakes. She was digging in with gusto. I supposed working several jobs and being up early to do one of those jobs would leave a person hungry.

I took my first bite and was pleasantly surprised. Her eyes lit up. "What do you think?" she asked excitedly. "Amazing, right?"

"They are pretty good."

"Liar," she laughed. "I can see the joy on your face. They are amazing. I would venture to say they are the best you've ever had."

She wasn't wrong. "They're good," I repeated.

She laughed and took another bite. "You're a horrible liar. But that's okay. I know they are the best. I've eaten a lot of pancakes in my day, and you can't beat these."

"Fine," I conceded after tearing through half the stack. "They are the best."

Her face lit up. "Told you."

"What did you say your other job was?" I asked.

"Coffee shop," she answered. "It's one of the hot spots."

"Do you work full time?"

"No. Not at that job. I mean, if you add up all my jobs, it's probably two full-time jobs."

"That's a lot to keep up with," I said.

"It is, but I like it," she answered. "Okay, like might be a strong word, but I don't hate it. I like to stay busy. And I just keep thinking I'm planning ahead for the future. Eventually, all the work will pay off."

She was motivated. I had to give her that. It was an admirable quality. I wanted to ask a hundred more questions, but women could get skittish around strangers. I didn't want to freak her out. She didn't need to worry that I was a stalker.

I focused on the food. I had not eaten since the plane. I was starving, and the meal was amazing. I plowed through most of it and suddenly realized I was very full. "Wow," I said.

She was dabbing at her mouth. "I told you it was good."

"It was, and now I'm not sure if I can walk out of here," I joked. "I might need a stretcher."

She laughed again. "A good breakfast can make the entire day better. It can make you forget all your troubles."

"I'm not sure it's quite that powerful, but I do feel better," I admitted. "Thank you."

"You're very welcome. It was worth it to see you smile. I knew you had one in there."

"I'm sorry I wasn't very nice last night," I said.

"Or this morning," she pointed out.

My smile widened. "Yes. I apologize for that as well."

"No worries." She smiled. "It's your first full day here. You are officially started off on the right foot."

"Thank you," I said again. "I do feel much better about the day."

Makana came by with the check. Ava reached for it, but I was faster. "I offered to take you to breakfast," she said.

"You saved my ass," I told her with a shrug. I grabbed my wallet and pulled out a credit card. "The least I can do is buy you breakfast. My day was going to shit in a hurry. Thank you for saving me."

"You're very welcome," she said.

I paid the bill, making sure to leave a healthy tip. I was planning on coming back again. I wanted the same good service. She drove me back to the house with the Porsche sitting in the driveway. It looked fine. I hoped it wasn't damaged.

"Thank you," I said. "I won't bother you again. It sounds like you've got a full plate already."

"Call me anytime," she said. "Seriously, I don't mind helping out. I'm just a phone call away."

I headed inside, turning to wave when she honked her horn. Breakfast was good. The company was even better. I felt refreshed. Revived and ready for a day of doing nothing.

I woke up early the following morning. The temptation to treat myself to more of those pancakes was strong. But I couldn't eat like that every day. It would kill me. It was a whole lot of sweetness. I wasn't used to sweetness in the morning. I made my coffee instead and grabbed a yogurt from the fridge. My phone had been off since yesterday, and I didn't want to turn it on. I was pretty sure it would just be more of the same. My keys and wallet were sitting on the counter with the receipt from yesterday's breakfast on top. Seeing her again seemed like a really good idea.

I remembered the name of her coffee shop and turned on my phone. I ignored the icons indicating I had voicemails and texts. I was only interested in finding her place. I felt like having some good coffee. And if I got to see her again, it wouldn't be the worst thing in the world. She had given me such a good start to my day yesterday. I knew she was busy, but if I could just talk to her for a couple of minutes, it might have the same effect.

Chapter Eight

Ava

"You be a good girl," I said to Roxy. "I have to work the coffee shop, and then we need to clean this house."

I picked up my shoes and tossed them in the room. I hated going to work and leaving my house a mess. It was just one of those things that irritated the hell out of me. When I was at work, all I could think about was the mess waiting for me at home. I whipped through the house, putting away this and that and neatly stacking the dirty dishes in the sink to be dealt with later.

The back door was open so Roxy could run in and out while I finished picking up. It was just after five. I actually got to sleep in for the morning. I was working a later shift, which I liked and hated. I liked being up early and getting off before lunch. It left me my whole day. Usually, my day would be spent at the big house working on the renovations. It felt strange not to have that on my plate. Once Ethan was gone, I was going to get back to work on it.

"Roxy, I have to go!" I shouted, knowing she would hear me in the backyard.

I waited a couple of minutes. She rushed inside and hopped on the couch, turning three times before settling into her spot. I patted her on the head and grabbed my purse. I drove to work with my favorite music on nice and loud. The streets were still pretty empty, something else I loved about working early. I didn't have to fight traffic.

I slipped in the back door and put my things in the breakroom. It was still very quiet. Cindy was carrying a case of cups up front. "Good morning," I greeted her.

"Good morning," she smiled. "Lana called in sick. It's just us for an hour."

I noticed a couple of the regulars already seated and sipping their coffee. I pulled on my apron, quickly tying it in the back before I got busy stocking things before the morning rush.

"How's the rental property?" she asked while starting fresh coffee. "Any major problems?"

"Nope." I shook my head. "So far, so good. Although he did get stuck in the mud yesterday. I had to bail him out. It seemed like it was going to ruin his day. I fixed him up with some of Makana's macadamia nut pancakes."

"That will cure anyone's bad day," she laughed. "Did you deliver the breakfast?"

"Nope, I took him," I said nonchalantly.

"Wait, you took a guy to breakfast?" she asked with surprise.

"I drove him there, but he paid." I shrugged. "He was thanking me for saving him."

"Is he an older guy?" she asked.

"No."

"College kid?" she asked and stepped closer.

I slowly shook my head. "No."

"Single?"

"Stop!" I laughed and went back to work. "He's just a renter. He's here by himself and seemed like he could really use some pancakes. That's it."

"Oh, girl." She shook her head. "That is most definitely not it. You're blushing."

"I'm not blushing," I argued.

Thankfully, I didn't have to answer any more questions and further embarrass myself. A group came in, and it was a steady stream of customers after that.

"Gavin!" I called out the name on one of the cups. Two guys stepped up to the counter. I inwardly groaned. Their cockiness was obvious. I just knew what was coming next.

"What time are you off work?" one asked me.

"Later." I smiled.

"Maybe you'd like to show us around your pretty little island," the other said.

"I'm sure you'll find nothing short of a hundred very willing tour guides around here," I told them.

"But we want you," the first insisted.

"Very sweet, but I'm busy," I said.

"Oh, come on now," one said. "We'll show you a good time."

"She's busy," I heard a familiar voice say.

Ethan stepped forward. He was taller and more intimidating than the two young bucks. There was a brief stare-down, and I wasn't sure what to think. The last person I expected to come to my rescue was Ethan.

"All right, man," one of the guys said. "Chill. We were just having some fun."

"Have fun somewhere else," Ethan growled.

The guys walked away, and I looked at Ethan with amusement. "Thank you."

"Sure. I've always hoped I would have the opportunity to help out a damsel in distress."

"What are you doing here?" I asked.

He shrugged. "I don't know," he answered. "You said I could call you if I needed anything. You said you would show me around if I wanted. Are you available?"

I couldn't help my grin. "I can be. I've got about another half hour on my shift. Did you want to go today?"

"That would be great." He nodded. "I'll order a cup of coffee."

He walked to the end of the line. He was wearing jeans and a T-shirt and he hadn't shaved again. Cindy was watching me along with the other two girls. I felt my cheeks burning. "What?" I asked innocently.

"Who's the hottie?" Cindy whispered close to my ear.

"Stop it," I hissed. "He's my client."

"The guy renting the new house?"

"Yes." I nodded. I glanced up once to find him watching me. I was mortified. I was sure he knew we were talking about him. It felt very high school.

"He's hot," one of the girls said. "Like super-hot."

I ignored them and made the next order. It was so hard not to look at him. He had his hands in the pockets of his jeans and looked so casual. He looked very different than the man I had met the first night he was in town. I was digging the scruffy face. He should keep that look. It worked for him.

He ordered his coffee—just coffee. I handed it to him with a smile. He sat down to drink it while all the other girls and I stared at him. We tried not to make it obvious, but I was pretty sure he saw us. I imagined he was used to it. He had to know he was serious eye candy.

After my shift, I joined him in the lobby area. "Ready?"

"I am," he said.

"I need to run by my place and let my dog out," I said. That was true, but it wasn't the only truth. I wanted to freshen up and change out of my uniform. I could smell the coffee clinging to me.

"Should I follow you?" he asked.

That's when it dawned on me I was talking about taking him to my place. Was that really what I wanted to do? I tried to remember if my bras were hanging over the shower curtain rod. Was the place a mess? I supposed it didn't matter. It wasn't like I had to impress him.

"Sure," I said.

I led him to my apartment and prayed like hell there was nothing too terrible laying around the house. I pushed the door open. "Watch for Roxy," I warned three seconds before she came bounding down the hall.

"Hey, girl," I greeted her. "She's harmless," I assured him.

He looked a little awkward. "Hello, Roxy," he said.

I walked to the kitchen and refilled her water bowl. "Roxy, come on, let's go outside."

I walked to the back door and opened it to let her out. "I'm going to change really quick," I said to Ethan, who was still standing in the living room.

"I'll be here," he said.

I rushed into my bedroom and closed the door. I stepped in front of the mirror and grimaced. I really needed a quick makeover. I didn't want to make him wait while I showered, which meant a quick sponge bath to hit the hot spots. I tore off my uniform and grabbed a washcloth. I couldn't believe he had shown up, since I had only casually mentioned where I worked. It was exciting to have a man like him come by and want to talk to me.

I spritzed on some fruity body spray, brushed out my hair, and then quickly touched up my makeup. If I dressed like I was going on a date, he was going to think I was trying to impress him. This was just a casual thing. I wasn't going to fool myself into thinking he wanted anything more than a tour guide. I was the only person on the island that he knew. I had a feeling he wasn't the kind of person that made friends easily. I was the easiest option because I'd put myself in his orbit whether he liked it or not.

I scanned my closet and pulled out a fun blouse. I stuck with the usual jeans, and instead of booties, I put on my favorite wedges. It wasn't a lot, not date-ready, but better than the bland coffee shop uniform. It was a fine line. I didn't want to try too hard, but I didn't want to not try at all. Ethan was an attractive man. I didn't want to be the frumpy tour guide leading him around.

I knew there was no chance of anything happening between us. He was the kind of guy that dated princesses and A-list Hollywood stars. Supermodels would clamor to get to him. I might not be the kind of woman he would go out with, but I wasn't opposed to being his friend. He seemed like he could use a friend. The man was very closed off. Just the fact he was here by himself staying in my house away from the tourist traps told me he was hiding. He had a story. While I was curious about what that story was, I wouldn't pry. If he wanted to talk, I would be a listening ear. I felt like that was something I was good at. Life had put me through my paces. I knew what it was like to feel alone. To feel like hiding on an island was the only way to get through life. He was just my renter, but I didn't mind offering some free advice.

If I could help one person, I was going to feel like I had done something good. So many people had helped me over the last few years. I saw someone that could use a break from whatever it was he was dealing with back home. It was a good lesson in not judging a book by its cover. Yes, he was wealthy. Yes, he probably had enough money to buy whatever he wanted, but happiness was not for sale. I had seen it first-hand. I knew plenty of wealthy, miserable people.

I was going to keep my mouth shut and not pry. If he was having problems with a wife or girlfriend, I had no business wading into that. Simply spending time with me might make the situation worse. A lonely man far away from his significant other could be dangerous. I refused to be the other woman. I would be a listening ear and maybe even a shoulder to lean on, but I would not let it go any further than that.

Chapter Nine

Ethan

I walked into the small living room that was open to the dining room and the kitchen. It was all very small. A single couch and a chair in the corner crowded the space. Her TV was on a small stand in the corner. I had stayed in larger hotel rooms. Her place was all very normal. The kind of place I saw in TV shows. I couldn't remember ever actually seeing an average home. My life had been one of privilege. My friends were all from wealthy families. A family home with only six bedrooms was considered small. It was like a museum display for me, but I wasn't going to tell her that.

There were lots of pictures on the wall and set up on small tables. There was one man that was dominant in most of the photos. I assumed it was her father. He looked very vibrant. A real outdoorsman. There were pictures of him out on the water surfing, fishing, and driving boats. Several pictures included Ava. I wondered if she had been raised by a single father.

I looked at another picture that was much bigger. It was the same man by himself. Once again, he was on a boat with a dolphin leaping out of the water behind him. A thought occurred, one that didn't quite sit right with me. What if it wasn't her father but a boyfriend? It wouldn't be unheard of for a woman to date an older man. It was certainly common enough in my world.

The back door was still open, which I assumed she did on purpose. I sat down to wait for her to finish changing. Her house was very comfortable. It felt homey. Again, it reminded me of the kind of homes I saw on television sitcoms. My own childhood home had been huge.

The couches were always stiff. Everything felt new. Just when things started to get broken in, they were taken away and replaced with something new. Maybe it was the novelty of the place, but I liked it.

I was lost in thought when the dog hopped up on the couch. It stared at me for several seconds, and I began to wonder if it was about to attack me. I searched my brain to remember the name of the beast. "Hello, Roxy," I said gently.

The dog leaned forward and sniffed. I didn't dare move. I wasn't sure if I should kick it off the couch or what. Then, as if I passed a test, it flopped down beside me with its head resting on my lap. The dog let out a long sigh and seemed to fall asleep almost immediately. I didn't dare move.

"Okay," Ava said.

I looked at her, waiting to see if I was in trouble for letting the dog on the couch. She paused halfway down the hall and looked at me and the dog. I was definitely in trouble. She had let her hair down and put on a little makeup. The tight jeans she'd put on showed off her long legs. I was attracted to her. The realization hit me hard. Obviously, she was a beautiful woman, but I didn't actually expect to be attracted to her.

"Is this bad?" I asked.

She smiled and walked around to face us. She stood in front of me, and I was able to get a much better look at her. Why hadn't I noticed how attractive she was before? Technically, I had, but that side of me had been pretty much dead. At least until about thirty seconds ago. Now it was alive and well, and there was a stirring inside, like my body was just coming out of hibernation. I supposed in some ways it was. I had been working so damn hard, I didn't have time for women. No women meant no sex. The worst part about all of that was I actually hadn't missed it. Until now.

"Not bad." Ava smiled. "Roxy, what are you doing?"

The dog didn't move. "She seemed like she knew what she was doing," I said.

"Oh, she does," Ava laughed. "I'm just not used to seeing her be so comfortable with strangers. She's usually very suspicious of new people. I got her from a shelter a couple of years ago. I don't know what she had gone through in her life, but she took to me right away, but that was it. It usually takes her some time before she warms up to anyone."

"I've never thought of myself as a dog person, but maybe I am." I shrugged.

Ava sat down with Roxy between us and rubbed the dog's back. "Roxy knows good people."

"Thanks."

"So there's a pub I think you would like," she said. "They serve some of the best burgers. The fries are homemade."

"A pub?" I asked.

"Bar. Tavern. A watering hole. The name is Duke's Pub, so I think that makes it a pub. The guy moved here thirty years ago from Ireland. He has a unique selection of beer made right here in Hawaii."

"Are there chickens in the front?" I asked with a smile.

"Not always," she replied. "It's not fancy with lots of LED lighting and a bunch of bells and whistles. It's a place a lot of the Navy guys like to hang out at. You're not going to find too many tourists there."

"Ah, ugly on the outside." I nodded.

"You could say that," she agreed.

"You were right about the pancakes, so I'll trust your judgment," I said. "It's definitely a different way to see the place."

"You're getting to see the cool spots most tourists will never see," she said. "The places that are the true heart and soul of this island paradise."

"I bet it's obnoxious playing host to thousands of people every month," I said.

She shrugged. "Not really. It gets a little crowded, but without those people coming every month, a lot of us would be in dire straits. I guess you could say it's a double-edged sword."

"I get it." I nodded.

"We should get going," she said. "I would hate for you to get hangry."

"How do you know I haven't eaten already?" I asked.

She looked at me with her brows raised. "Something tells me you aren't used to making your own meals."

She wasn't wrong. "I can make my own meals."

"But do you?" she asked. "And did you really come all the way here to slave over a hot stove when there is a perfectly good burger waiting for you? Not just a burger but home-brewed beer. Live a little."

"Okay." I shrugged. "I'll drive, assuming we're not going off-roading."

"I promise it is paved all the way there," she laughed. "It's about twenty minutes away. Are you okay with that?"

"Very."

Ava patted Roxy on the butt and got to her feet. I didn't move. Roxy didn't seem inclined to move her head from my lap. She really did look comfortable. I didn't want to disturb her.

Ava started laughing. "Roxy, get down," she ordered. "Just give her a nudge, she'll move."

I felt terrible for disturbing the dog. I got up and brushed off the dog hair. Ava closed the back door and grabbed her purse. That was something I could really get used to about living in Hawaii. I didn't have to put on a restricting coat, scarf, gloves, and the works. It was very easy to leave the house.

I opened the passenger door for her out of habit. When I got into the driver's seat, she was running her hand over the leather seat. "Nice," she said with a nod. "I can see why you wanted to take your car."

"I had grand plans to go for a long drive around the island with the top down."

"And you don't anymore?" she asked.

"I suppose I do, but I'm just not sure about the rain," I answered.

"There are plenty of days full of nonstop sunshine. I think you'll find it's a very relaxing ride. Assuming you don't encounter some of our famous traffic. That's kind of a pain in the ass."

"I've noticed," I said. "All right, where are we going?"

"Take a left," she said. "Just follow the road to the main drag and keep going toward Pearl City."

I did what she said. The sun was out, and it seemed like a waste not to put the top down. I pushed a button and let it fold down. Ava put her hands in the air. "See! Can you just feel your worries evaporating under the sun?"

I liked her ability to be carefree. She didn't have much, but she had it all. She had told me to choose happiness. I understood why she was happy. She chose to be despite not having a lot. I liked that she didn't seem to care who I was. She was living in the moment. I wanted that. It was freeing. I could be me, Ethan, without being Ethan Mitchell CEO.

I glanced over at her as the car sped down the highway. I wondered if she knew who I was. Was she pretending she didn't just to get me to let down my guard? I didn't think so. I had been around women and men who wanted me to think they were very cool and casual with who I was. Usually, it ended up being a ploy. They pretended they didn't care that I had a ton of money because they thought it would put me at ease. Unfortunately, my guard was always up. In New York, few people didn't know who I was. My family had put me in the spotlight at a young age. People wanted to get close to me because they thought I would give them an advantage in life. My connections. My money. My company. There was always an angle.

"Take a right up here!" she shouted loudly enough to hear over the wind blowing through our hair.

That was something else I appreciated about her. She was very natural. Her hair was whipping around her face, but she didn't seem to care. The fact it could whip around was also impressive. A lot of the women I had dated put enough product in their hair to stop a bullet. Not Ava.

I felt my stress melting away. I could just relax. I could let my guard down and not worry that someone was going to take my picture or ask me for anything. It was a strange feeling to feel safe. Not safe from danger, but safe from people wanting something from me. People hoping and waiting for me to screw up so they could document it. My muscles felt looser. I didn't have the furrowed brow I normally did.

This was what I wanted out of life. It was why I had fled to Hawaii in the first place. I wanted to escape who I was back there and what that meant. I looked over at her and had to smile. While she was definitely not a dog, she reminded me of the joy I saw on a dog's face when they had their heads hanging out the window with their tongues lolling. She was truly happy.

"Another right," she said.

I followed her directions until we were at our destination. I put the top up, just in case it decided to rain. A man coming out of the pub waved at her. "Hey, Ava," he said. "How are you doing?"

She gave him a quick hug. "I'm good," she replied. "How are you?"

"Good, good." He nodded. "On my way to the store before the wife figures out I've been gone a little too long."

"You better get home," she scolded him, laughing.

I was beginning to think she was either a celebrity on the island or she was just the type of person everyone loved. I didn't miss the fact that most of the people who seemed to go out of their way to talk to her were older. I wondered if it had anything to do with the man in the photos. Maybe that's who she chose to spend her time with. But the way they all smiled at her and seemed to be checking on her told me otherwise. It gave me family vibes, like they were all part of an extended family.

Chapter Ten

Ava

We walked into the pub with the usual suspects sitting at the bar. The man behind the bar waved at me. I waved back and led Ethan to a table with high bench seats. They weren't necessarily comfortable, but they were original to the building, and they did give people a little privacy. There weren't going to be any little kids pulling at your hair or dropping stuff over.

"This is, uh, dark," he said.

"I told you there weren't any LEDs," I reminded him. "Just good greasy food and even better beer."

"I am actually looking forward to trying it," he said.

"I'm guessing you haven't eaten in a place like this before?" I asked with a grin.

"You would guess correctly." He nodded.

"Look at you," I teased. "You're trying all kinds of new things."

"When in Rome," he said.

"Hi, Ava," the waitress greeted us.

"Hi, Kali." I smiled. "We're going to need a menu. My friend would like to see what you have. Any good beers today?"

"Duke made his special batch," she said. "It's been going fast."

"We'll take two," I said.

"I'll be right back," Kali said. She returned a few seconds later and handed Ethan a menu.

"I think I'll just let you order for me," he said.

"It's pretty basic," I assured him. "Go ahead and look."

"Do they put pineapple on the burgers?" he asked.

"If you'd like them to," I laughed.

He scanned the menu. "I think I'll just stick with a cheeseburger."

"Me too." I nodded. "It'll come with mac salad and coleslaw. You can get fries if you'd like."

"Mac salad sounds good," he said.

Kali brought our beers in glass mugs. "What do you think?" I asked after he took his first drink.

"Different," he answered.

"Duke likes stout beers," I laughed. "We can get you something else."

"No, it's fine," he said.

"Have you been to Oahu before?" I asked him.

"Yes." He nodded. "Once. I've been to the big island a few times when I was younger."

"You're from New York?" I gently probed. I wanted to learn more about him. I told myself it was just to help him, but I was interested in learning more about the guy.

"Born and raised," he answered.

His answers were always stilted. I couldn't tell if it was because he didn't want to reveal anything or if he was just not used to small talk. Or maybe it was me. I wasn't from his world. Technically, I supposed I was, but I didn't feel like it. That was my old life. I wasn't the same Ava that had grown up in New York.

"Is your family still there?" I asked.

He nodded and sipped from the mug. "Yes."

I got the hint. He didn't want to talk about anything personal. Prying into his life was not what I wanted to do. "Do you have any plans while you're here?" I asked him. "Are you a history buff? Have you been to the Pearl Harbor Memorial?"

"I think I visited when I was a kid," he answered. "I don't remember it all that well. We might have flown over it."

It was hard for me to understand how someone could visit the place and not remember it, but I supposed he was far removed to what that meant to a lot of families on the island and around the world.

"I recommend touring it again," I said, maybe a little abruptly.

"Ava."

I looked up and saw one of my dad's old friends. "Captain." I smiled and got to my feet to give him a hug. "What are you doing in here in the middle of the day?"

He winked. "I'm taking some needed time off. How are you doing?"

"I'm good." I nodded.

"Good to hear," he said. "Trudy and I were thinking about you the other day. We promised your dad we would look in on you, and I realized it had been months since I saw you."

"I appreciate that," I said. "How is Trudy?"

"She got one of those Cricut machines," he said with a shake of his head. "My office is covered in things she's made with that thing. I've got coasters, bags, T-shirts and just about anything else you can think of."

I laughed at the idea of him wearing a T-shirt made by his wife. "She could make and sell stuff."

"Don't you dare tell her that," he groaned. "She's already taken over one room of the house. Everyone is getting something handmade for Christmas."

"I'm glad she's found something she loves," I said.

He glanced over at Ethan, then back at me. "I'll let you enjoy your meal. It was good to see you. You should come by the house. We'd love to have you over for dinner."

"I'll stop by," I promised.

"I'll be looking for you," he said and gave me another hug.

I sat down after he walked away. It still hurt to see my dad's friends happy and healthy. My dad always told me he'd pulled the short straw and that was that. It sucked. There were days I wanted to complain it wasn't fair. But I didn't because he didn't want me to. He told me if he didn't pull it, someone else would.

"Everything okay?" Ethan asked.

"Yes." I nodded and forced a smile.

"That was your father's friend?" he asked.

"Yes." Now I sounded like Ethan. I wasn't used to people not knowing my dad or his story. It was a sensitive subject, but it wasn't like it was a secret. What did it matter if Ethan knew? "His friends, Navy buddies, like to keep an eye on me. They all think of me as their own."

"Your dad was in the Navy?"

I smiled. "Yes. Twenty years. He was stationed here the last few years. When he retired, he decided to stay. He said he couldn't imagine living anywhere else. He was stationed here at the beginning of his career and then moved around quite a bit. As he moved up the ranks, he always put in to get back here. Unfortunately, by the time he got stationed back here, my parents were divorced, and we moved away."

"Past tense," he said.

"What?" I asked with confusion.

"You are talking about your father in the past tense."

"He passed away a few years ago," I said. "What's funny, but not really funny, was that it took me months to refer to him in the past tense. I was always talking about him like he was going to walk through the door or take me fishing. I cannot even count the number of times I called him or sent him a text."

"That must have been hard," he said.

I felt the melancholy coming on. I didn't want to be sad. I had spent plenty of time feeling like that. "It was, but that's when his buddies really stepped up. They took turns stopping by or calling me to see how I was doing. They are good people."

"You're fortunate to have had them," he said.

"I know. I am so grateful for them. I don't know how I would have gotten through it without them."

"Were you close?" he asked gently.

"Yes," I acknowledged. "But not always. It sucks because we had just finally gotten to know each other. I moved here right after I graduated college. I visited and decided to stay. He was my best friend. Then he got sick—lung cancer. It hit hard and fast. One day we were fishing, and he passed out. Thankfully, his friends were with us. We got him to the hospital, and our world changed. It was so crazy to think we went from celebrating to mourning. His friends—some are still in the Navy, but many are retired—they were amazing. They helped out and pretty much adopted me as their own."

"Because military sticks together," he stated.

"They do," I said with a sigh. "My dad was a good guy. He was solid. People recognized that. People were just drawn to him. He was loyal. His friends knew they could count on him. If it had been one of them that got sick, he would have taken care of their family. It's what they did."

"I was in the Air Force for four years," he announced.

"Really?" I asked with surprise. "You?" I was suddenly rethinking everything I'd initially thought about him. Maybe he wasn't rich. I felt terrible for judging him. I assumed he was the kind of guy that had been born with money. Now I wondered if he had made his money the old-fashioned way.

"Yes." He shrugged. "I would have re-upped, but family obligations pulled me back. I loved my time in the Air Force. I made a lot of good friends. Unfortunately, I wasn't in long enough to have made lifelong friends. I talk to a few of the guys now and then, but I always felt like a quitter for leaving."

"There are plenty of people who only do a four-year stint," I said. "You're not a quitter."

"Thanks."

"I knew there was something about you," I laughed. "I've always been drawn to the military type."

"Man in a uniform?" he said with a laugh. "I don't think there are many women that can resist that."

"Well, yes and no," I said. "I'm surrounded by men in uniform. It's not the uniform, it's the man that wears it."

"I see," he said. "Honor and all that."

"Something like that," I agreed. "I think I've been lucky to meet a lot of chivalrous men. Then again, I've met plenty of men in uniform that are not so chivalrous."

"Drunken sailors?" he joked.

"Yes." I nodded. "Drunken Marines, soldiers, you name it."

"I can only imagine given the number stationed just on this one small island," he said.

"Do you still have your uniform?" I asked curiously. I didn't know why I asked. But I imagined he looked hot in it. Really hot.

He raised an eyebrow. "Are you hoping to see it?"

He was funny. I knew there was a sense of humor under that tough exterior. "Sorry, buddy, but you can save that for someone else," I laughed. "But I wouldn't hate to see a picture of you in it."

"Just say the word." He winked. "I'll have it mailed to me."

I rolled my eyes. "I think a picture will do."

He was flirting. Not that he was great at it, but he was trying. That was a lot better than the way he had been. I loved watching the layers fall away. A few more days and he would be actually laughing. I was going to make sure he had a good time on his vacation.

"What'd you do in the Air Force?" I asked.

"I would love to tell you I was a pilot, but I was an analyst," he said with disappointment. "I have a knack for seeing patterns, and I'm pretty savvy with computers. Honestly, I didn't have any desire to be a pilot. A lot of guys thought that's what the Air Force was all about. They were pretty disappointed when they discovered very few actually got to sit in a cockpit."

"Every job is important, even if it doesn't come with a lot of fanfare," I said.

"Thanks."

"I'm serious," I insisted. "All jobs are necessary."

"It was a long time ago," he said. "My ego has recovered."

Chapter Eleven

Ethan

I figured I should change the subject. I saw the sadness in her eyes when she talked about her dad.

"Do you have more family here in Oahu or one of the other islands?" I asked.

"No," she answered.

Our food was delivered, and for a few minutes, we didn't talk while we ate. I reached for a napkin and wiped my mouth while nodding. "Good," I murmured.

"Told you." She grinned.

I took a few more bites before I finally managed to put down the burger and come up for air. "You said your family isn't here. Are they, well, you know?"

"They are not dead." She said it with a laugh, which made me feel a lot better. I felt guilty for intruding. "They live in New York."

"Really?" I asked with shock. "Did you live in New York?"

"Yes." She nodded. "When my parents split, my mom took me and my sister to New York to live with her family."

"I had no idea you were from New York," I said. "You don't have a New Yorker attitude."

"And that's why I moved here," she said. "I didn't belong there. I always felt out of place. The moment I came back here, I knew it was where I belonged."

"Do you see them?" I asked.

"No." She shook her head. "We're not close. We're the opposite of close."

I saw the darkness. I felt that same darkness whenever I thought about my family. "I get that," I muttered.

"I haven't seen them in years, and to be perfectly honest, that does not make me sad," she said. "I should know better after losing so much time with my dad, but I just haven't been able to bring myself to care."

"Trust me," I said, nodding, "I get it. I'm not on the best terms with my family either."

"Which explains why you are here alone."

"Bingo," I replied.

She took another bite of her burger. There was an expression on her face that looked like she was trying to make a decision. "My family was pissed when I came out here," she said. "Then when I told my mom and sister he was sick, it was like they didn't care. My family had money. They could have helped. They rejected my pleas. They completely abandoned me and him. My dad was fortunate to have the bulk of his medical covered, but that didn't help when he couldn't work. I had to keep a roof over our heads and buy the things he needed to be comfortable. I was so glad he lived much longer than the doctors said he would, but the financial burden was pretty heavy. I'm still paying it off."

"That's why you work so many jobs," I said.

"Yep." She shrugged. "But I got the last laugh."

"How so?"

"The Mitchells," she grinned.

My heart skipped a beat. "What?"

"My mother's family thought they were all high and mighty," she said. "They were tight with their money. They had so much of it, but they refused to help me out. I understood why my mom might not want to help out her ex-husband, but it was for me. I was paying the mortgage and everything else. She was so spiteful. Then the Mitchell family came along and made sure I would never get a penny from my family."

There was a buzzing in the back of my mind. Did she know who I was? Was that what all of this was about? Was she trying to make me pay for whatever crime my family had committed against hers? I was suddenly uncomfortable. I tried to place her name. I didn't remember any companies with the name Hunt attached. I wondered if her family owned a company we'd acquired in a hostile takeover. Or maybe they were employed by a company we'd taken over and dissolved. It was hard to say, which said a lot about my life. How many lives had I ruined? So many I couldn't even count them all.

"Your family lost their money?" I asked.

"Yes, you are very lucky you are not one of those Mitchells," she said with a laugh. "We would have to be sworn enemies."

I guess that answered a few of my questions. She didn't realize I was one of them. I didn't think she was lying. There was an honesty about her that couldn't be faked. That meant I was going to be lying to her face. A lie by omission was still a lie.

I made a noise of acknowledgement and quickly took a big bite to have an excuse why I couldn't keep talking. She took another bite of her burger.

"I believe in karma," she said when she swallowed it. "I think my mom got exactly what she deserved. My dad was a good man. He was too good to leave my mother. She left him. I think it stemmed from him wanting to stay in the Navy. Mom wanted her mansion and fast cars. My dad's salary wasn't enough for her. I think she had some kind of rebellious streak when she married him. Then when she got bored, she left. My sister and I didn't get a choice in the matter. One day we were a family, and the next we were on a plane to New York."

"Have you had any kind of contact with your mother since your father died?"

She shook her head. "No. My sister calls on occasion, but we don't really talk. She could have come to see our father before he died, but she didn't. I can't imagine what kind of guilt she will have for the rest of her days. I tried to tell her, but she didn't want to listen. I don't wish that on her, but I hope she feels some regret."

"You took care of your father?" I asked.

"Yes," she replied. "My dad was a Navy man. He didn't want to be in a hospital. He wanted to be in his own house in his own bed. I wasn't able to do much for him, but I could give him that much. He was very proud and hated the idea of a nurse coming in. Thankfully, his friends stepped up. They never let him feel like a burden. Even on his last day, they came over to have a beer with him. They kept it normal for him. I am so very grateful for that. For them. Their families. All of them."

"That's a lot for one person to take on," I said. "You don't seem very old. Twenty-four? Twenty-five?"

"Flattery will get you everywhere," she laughed. "I'm twenty-eight."

"Still young," I said.

"What about you?" she asked. "You have the eyes of an old man, but you definitely don't look old."

"I feel old," I said with a sigh. "I'm thirty-seven, but when I say I feel like ninety, I'm not joking."

"You need more time on the beach," she said with a smile. "It keeps you young. Stress makes you feel old. It's not good for you."

"I know," I agreed. "I don't want to be stressed. I guess that's why I'm here. I need to get away from the drama."

"Your family is still in New York?" she guessed.

"Yes," I answered. I was afraid to say too much. I didn't want her to figure out I was a part of the family she loathed. I didn't know if I could call her a friend, but I didn't want to risk losing her. She was good. She was the kind of person that made the world better.

"You reserved my house for a month. Are you going back to them after your stay here?" she asked.

"I don't think I can answer that just yet," I said. "I have to. I know I do, but I'm not sure I want to. No, that's not true. I know I don't want to. I don't know what I want exactly, but I know I can't keep going the way I have been."

"This is a great place to do some soul searching," she said. "I came here right before I went to college. I wanted to stay then, but he insisted I go to school. When I came back after graduation, I wasn't in a great place. I hated college. I barely graduated. I knew I didn't want to be in New York, but I didn't know what I wanted. My dad basically unplugged me from the world for a week. We did nothing but hang out on the beach, surf, fish, and look at the stars. After a week, it was clear. I knew what I wanted to do. I went back and packed the rest of my things and moved out here."

"You lived with your dad?"

"For a month, then I got my own place. I was working online and making okay money, but when my dad got sick, I realized I had slipped back into that part of my life I was trying to get away from." She finished her beer. "Money wasn't the most important thing in the world. Happiness was. I made changes. Despite being incredibly sad, I am very happy."

"You're—" I stopped myself. I almost told her she was incredible, but I didn't want to come on too strong.

"I'm—?" she asked.

"You're very wise for your age," I said.

"I guess that makes two of us," she laughed.

"I have a proposal," I said. It was probably a bad idea, but the words were already out of my mouth.

"That sounds interesting."

"So far, you've shown me two really great places," I said. "You're taking me to the parts of the island I would probably never see if it weren't for you. I've been to all the islands, but I've never gotten to see what it's like for the people that live here. I bet you know all the coolest places."

"Damn straight I do." She grinned.

"I'd like to hire you."

She raised an eyebrow. "Hire me?"

"To be my personal tour guide," I clarified. "Show me around the island. I'll pay you. I don't want to visit the hottest beaches. I've been there, done that. I want to see what you see. I want to go where you go when you're off work. Where you go with your friends. I've seen all the cool stuff."

She mulled it over. "I can't charge you for that."

"Sure you can," I insisted. "I could pay a tour guide and not get even half the experience you could give me. I know you know this place like the back of your hand. I want to pay you to give me the full experience."

"It's too weird," she protested.

"How many jobs do you have?" I asked.

"Three."

"Are you close to getting out of debt?" I questioned.

She snorted. "No."

"And when you're not working one job, you're working another, right?" I pressed on.

"Yes," she said. "Or I'm working on the house, but I can't do that right now. I've got a guest."

"If you're not at work and you're not painting, then you would still be trying to make money. I'm offering to pay you. I can't keep taking advantage of your time. If you don't take my money, then we can't keep sharing these meals together. I'll feel too guilty. I don't want you to miss out on a moneymaking opportunity."

She sighed. "I'm not broke."

"I didn't mean to imply you were, but seriously, I'm asking a lot of you," I said. "I would feel better if I could compensate you. Please. If you're too busy, I understand."

"I'm not too busy," she said. "Can I have a minute to think about it?"

"Sure."

When the check came, I took it once again. "You don't have to keep buying me meals," she said.

"Consider it a bribe," I teased.

"A bribe?"

"I'm hoping to convince you to be my personal tour guide," I said. "This is me bribing you."

She laughed and shook her head. "You drive a hard bargain."

"I know."

Chapter Twelve

Ava

I sat quietly on the way back to my place. My normal reaction was to turn down payment for anything that should be given freely. However, I needed the money, and he was the kind of man that would not want to take anything for free. It was a pride thing. I understood it because my dad was the same way. It would be nice to hang out with him. I was enjoying getting to know him.

He was a hard man to read. I could see him slowly dropping that shell he'd put up around himself. I believed him when he said he wanted to see the true beauty of the island. Part of me was worried this little stint was something like what my mother went through when she hooked up with my father. The rich liked to play in the real world. They thought it was a game. When they were done seeing how the other half lived, they went back to their lives.

But there was something genuine about him. He could be putting on a show, but I didn't think so. Paying me would be nothing for him. And it would be a lot for me. It would be a win-win situation. He parked his car next to mine.

"You've been awful quiet," he said.

"I've been thinking."

"If I've made you uncomfortable, I'm sorry," he said.

"Do you want to come in for a minute?" I asked. "We can discuss your proposal."

"Sounds good." He smiled.

"Watch out for Roxy," I warned.

I let Roxy out and then joined him in the kitchen. He had his hands in his front pockets, staring at the picture of me and my dad at the beach. "That's him?"

"Yes." I nodded. "That's my dad."

"Are you going to reject my request?" he asked. "You can just say it."

"No, but I would like to clarify a few things," I said. "How often do you want to go out?"

He shrugged. "I'll take you as often as you can."

"Are you serious about wanting to see everything?"

"I am." He nodded. "If I'm not out sightseeing, I'm going to think I should work. I'm a workaholic. When I'm not working, I'm thinking about work. It's not good for my new stress-free existence."

"You're teasing," I accused him.

"Not at all," he said with a shake of his head. "You've distracted me in the best way. I can seriously feel my blood pressure go down."

I laughed. "I believe it. Okay, I can maybe do a couple hours a day. Does that work for you?"

"It does." He nodded. "I'll take what I can get. How about I pay you five hundred a day?"

"Stop," I said. "That's ridiculous."

"A thousand?"

"No. That is way too much money. How about fifty dollars?"

"I cannot pay you fifty bucks," he scoffed like he was insulted.

"I can't take a thousand."

He looked thoughtful. "How about three hundred? I can't go any lower."

It was the strangest negotiation. He was trying to get me to take more money than I thought my services were worth. "Fine, but for what it's worth, I think that's too much. I would be happy to take you around without you paying me."

"I know you would, but I don't like using people, and if I don't pay for your time, I will be using you," he said. "Please, let me pay you. Consider it me donating to a fellow military guy."

"You're very good," I said. "I bet you get your way a lot."

"I do." He grinned.

"When do you want to start?" I asked him.

He shrugged. "Are you free tomorrow?"

I thought about it and then nodded. "I am."

"Then I'll be ready," he said.

"I'll let you know what time," I said.

He looked around my place again. I got the impression he was stalling. "Do you want to go with me to walk a couple of dogs?" I offered.

He smiled and shook his head. "Thank you, but I've taken enough of your time. I'm going to head back to the house. First, I'm going to pick up some groceries because contrary to what you might think, I can put a frozen pizza in the oven."

I laughed. "Understood. I can't tell you what not to do, but don't work if you don't absolutely have to. Sit on the deck with a cold beer and enjoy the sunset. Take a breath. Turn off the TV and just be in the moment."

"I will do that," he said.

"Liar."

"Okay, I'll try to do that," he corrected. "It's hard for me to turn off. I guess that's why I'm here. I tried to rent an island, but then I remembered I don't cook."

"You could have packed a bunch of frozen pizzas," I suggested.

"But I would get very bored," he said. "I'm used to constant input."

I didn't know why I did it, but I reached out and touched his arm. "Trust me when I say this, unplugging will do wonders for you. I know how hard it is. When my dad suggested it, I was one of those girls on social media all the time. It was so weird to not have my phone on me."

"I've noticed you don't keep a phone on you," he said.

I pulled my hand back. "I do, but it's usually on silent. I want to live in the moment. Once you're rid of that damn albatross around your neck, you're going to feel free. You strike me as a guy used to constant phone calls and texts. No matter where you are, you're still at work. Even here."

"Everything you're saying is true," he admitted. "I know that. I am doing my best to pull back. With you showing me around, it's going to help me unplug."

"Challenge accepted." I smiled. "You're going to be so distracted with the beauty of this place, you're going to forget you have a job at all."

"If that's possible, I'm all in."

"Thank you for lunch," I said. "You're good company."

"I think you are probably the only person on this planet that has ever said that," he laughed. "I haven't been good company in a long time."

"You're doing just fine," I assured him. "Are you sure you can find your way back?"

"Are you teasing me?"

"Maybe a little, but I don't want you to get lost," I said.

"I know what road not to take," he said. "I'll be fine. Thank you. I'll see you tomorrow."

I walked him to the door and waved as he pulled away. Then I closed the door and leaned against it. "Oh Ava, what are you doing?"

I needed to keep a clear head about this. Ethan needed a friend. A temporary friend. Nothing more. It didn't matter that I got butterflies in my belly just thinking about spending time with him. I pushed away the romantic thoughts and reminded myself this was a job.

I grabbed a notepad and pen and headed out back to make a list of the places I wanted to show Ethan. There were so many. I jotted down a couple of my dad's fishing spots. My dad knew the island better than anyone. I'd been lucky enough to have him act as my tour guide. He'd shown me so many amazing places. Some of them I wanted to hold near and dear to my heart because they were so special. They were places I went to when I was missing him. I wasn't sure I wanted to let a man that was virtually a stranger into my world.

I jotted down a couple of the places, just in case I changed my mind. Something told me Ethan would appreciate the natural beauty. It would help heal his soul. He was in the same shape I had been in all those years ago when I'd shown up at my dad's door with two suitcases.

"Roxy, come on, girl!" I got to my feet and walked into the house.

Roxy followed behind me. I put some food in her bowl and went to take a shower. Now that I had let myself think about Ethan in the light of a man and not a renter, I couldn't stop thinking about it. The last thing I needed in my life was a vacation romance. A lot of other people that lived here didn't mind the short-term flings. In fact, many people actually liked the no-strings thing. There were no messy breakups or hurt feelings. Once the person's vacation was over, the relationship was over. I did try it once. It just wasn't for me. It was weird to date for a week and then never see each other again. I wasn't sure I was cut out for it.

That's why I could not let myself think about Ethan as anything more than a client. He was someone who needed a little help. I could do that. And only that. After my little mental pep talk, I got busy doing the dishes. My phone vibrated on the table. I would have ignored it, but I worried Ethan had gotten lost again.

I quickly dried my hands and reached for it. "Shit."

It wasn't Ethan. It was my sister. I hit the decline button and put the phone down. I didn't want to talk to her. She had burned that bridge. Maybe one day, we could be friends again, but I didn't see how we would get there. She'd burned me. She'd burned my father. I was still bitter about that. That side of my family had never done anything to help me or anyone. They looked out for themselves. Getting away from them was the best thing I could have done. I'd dodged a bullet. Yes, I'd lost a lot, but I'd also gained happiness and self-respect.

Some days I felt like I was an orphan. I was virtually alone in the world. At least when it came to blood relatives. My biological family wasn't a part of my life, but I had the people in Oahu that considered me one of theirs. I was so glad my father had been the man he was. His character was what made all these people want to take care of me. I was living under the umbrella of his bright light in the world. I hated that he wasn't here. I had so many regrets about the time I didn't get to spend with him, but I couldn't change any of that. It had happened, and I just had to hold on to the knowledge I'd gotten a couple of really good years with him.

Chapter Thirteen

Ethan

I heard a noise but ignored it. It was still dark out, which meant it was way too early to get out of bed. I pulled the pillow under me and started to fall back to sleep when I heard another noise. That didn't seem right.

"Ethan." I heard a soft whisper.

I went perfectly still. My eyes popped open. Either I was having a weird dream or someone was in the house. Then I heard heavy breathing and footsteps. I reached out to turn on the lamp. I didn't get it on before a beast hopped on the bed and licked my face.

"What the fuck?" I pushed it away and turned on the light. That's when I saw a dog staring at me. I was certain it was smiling at me with its tongue hanging out. I rubbed my faced and tried to figure out if I was dreaming or if it was real.

"Roxy!"

Ava stepped into the doorway. "What is going on?" I asked with confusion. "Are you really here or is this a dream?"

"I'm so sorry," Ava said from the door. "Roxy, get over here right now!"

The dog hopped off the bed and sauntered over to stand next to Ava. "What's wrong?" I asked. I sat up, making sure the blanket was over my lap. Thank the Maker I didn't sleep in the nude. "Fire?"

"No." She shook her head. "I knocked and rang the bell. I didn't mean to intrude. I'm so, so sorry. I let myself in and was going to stay by the door, but Roxy took off up here."

I was slowly waking up. None of it felt real. "Okay, but why are you here? What time is it? Did I sleep through the day?"

"No, it's early," she said. "I thought we could start our sightseeing."

"Now?" I asked incredulously. "You want to go sightseeing now? What are we supposed to see? It's dark."

"Trust me, you'll want to see this." She smiled. "Can you be ready in about ten minutes? If not, we're going to miss it."

I was so confused. None of this made sense. I was obviously in a dream. I remembered going to bed thinking about her. This had to be the manifestation of those thoughts. I flopped back onto the bed. I waited to jerk awake for real. The dog's panting certainly sounded real.

I turned my head and saw them both still standing in the doorway watching me with the same confusion I felt. "We can try again tomorrow," Ava suggested.

"You're serious?" I asked.

"Yes." She smiled. "You said you want to see the spots the tourists don't know about. That's what I'm trying to do."

I sat up and threw off the blanket before remembering I was in my underwear. I didn't care. It wasn't like my dick was hanging out. "I'll get dressed," I muttered.

"Pants and a sweatshirt or light jacket," she said and rushed away like she was worried I might attack her.

I pulled on a pair of jeans before stumbling into the bathroom. I brushed my teeth, put on deodorant, and left it at that. I didn't have the time or desire to try and tame my hair. It was supposed to look messy. Usually it was a carefully sculpted messy. Now it was just straight-up messy.

I pulled on a shirt, found a sweatshirt, and headed downstairs with my shoes in hand. Ava was standing next to the front door. "I'm so sorry," she said again. "I did not mean to barge in on you while you were in bed. Roxy got away from me. She really likes you."

"It's fine," I mumbled. "It was a surprise."

"I'm so sorry," she repeated. "I'm so embarrassed."

"Why?" I shrugged while putting on my tennis shoes. "I was the one naked."

"Oh, God," she groaned. "I cannot believe I did that. I'm sorry."

"I'm sure you've seen it before," I said and got to my feet.

"Not exactly," I heard her mutter under her breath.

I followed her out of the house and to her car. She opened the back door and gestured for Roxy to hop in. I got into the passenger seat with my head leaned back. "I don't know if it makes a difference, but I brought coffee." She pointed to a to-go cup in the center console.

I quickly grabbed it. "It makes a huge difference."

She started down the road. It was just before dawn. The streets were empty. Everything was quiet. "Where are we going?" I asked her. "When I said I wanted to go sightseeing, I really thought we would be doing it in the daylight."

"I know." She nodded. "But this is something you're going to want to see, and it can only be seen first thing in the morning."

"I wasn't aware I was making a deal with a crazy person," I joked.

"You should have asked more questions," she laughed.

She parked her car on the side of the road in the middle of nowhere. "Ready?" she asked.

"No," I answered. "If I were a woman, and you were a dude, I would be very concerned. This is something out of a horror movie. What exactly do you plan on doing to me?"

"Stop," she giggled. "Take your coffee."

She opened the back door, and Roxy quickly hopped out. She had a flashlight in hand and shone it on a narrow trail that led up the mountain. It was chilly out, but not cold. She was wearing black leggings and a lightweight jacket. She walked ahead of me on the narrow trail, which gave me plenty of time to check out her fine ass.

Roxy was leading the way like they had done this walk many times before. We made it to the top fairly quickly. "Have a seat," Ava said and pointed to a large boulder.

"How long are we going to be out here?" I asked. "It's pretty damn cold."

"It's not that bad," she replied. "Besides, the cold is refreshing."

I sipped my coffee. "I could have been cold in New York."

"Man up," she scolded. "You're in the most beautiful place on earth, and you're about to see why."

I let out an audible sigh to show my frustration. "I take it you come up here often?"

"Not as often as I should," she replied. "I love it here."

"Alone?" I asked.

"Yes."

"Is that safe?" I questioned. "It was a goat trail up here. It's dark. I bet we don't have service up here. What if someone tries some shit?"

"I think you're a little too used to New York," she replied.

"I understand there might be less crime, but you're a woman, and it just doesn't seem safe for you to be roaming around in the dark by yourself," I said.

"I have Roxy," she replied. "Like I said, the only people that know about this place are locals. I trust my community."

I trusted almost no one. It was clear she loved her community and the island. "I appreciate that, but I just hope you let someone know when you're coming up here."

"You're sweet for caring," she said.

Daylight started to break. I got the impression she wanted silence. It felt like a reverent moment. Her gaze was straight ahead. Even Roxy was sitting quietly. I sipped my coffee and waited for whatever was going to happen. A gradual light began to spread out. Glorious yellows and oranges spread across the sky along with some billowing clouds.

The ocean reflected the colors, stirring them and creating a sherbet of blended color.

Neither of us talked. I understood the reverence. It was a moment that demanded complete attention. My breath hitched. I had never seen anything more beautiful. The sun ascended, and the pretty colors began to fade. The view was amazing.

"I get it," I said.

"Told you." She smiled up at me.

I didn't want to leave. I wasn't cold anymore. The sun was already warming the area. "Thank you for bringing me here. I really appreciate you sharing it with me."

"You're welcome."

"Sorry I was pissy," I said.

"It's understandable," she laughed. "You were woken up abruptly with a strange woman and a slobbering dog. Your irritability was warranted."

"It was a surprise," I admitted. "But a pleasant one."

"Have you been able to sleep okay at the house?" she asked.

"Yes," I answered. "It's been very comfortable."

"Good," she said. "That's the goal. I want my guests to be able to unwind and relax. It's a chance to get away from the stresses of the world."

"Can I ask you something?" I asked. "If it's intrusive, tell me to shut up."

"Shoot," she said. "I'll let you know."

"I know a little about real estate," I started. "Hawaii isn't cheap. The sheer size of the property tells me it's valuable. You said you've been doing some fixing up on the place, but it's not a dump. It couldn't have been cheap. I don't imagine you make that kind of money at the coffee shop. You'd have to walk a hundred dogs at once."

She laughed, which was a relief. I knew it was none of my business. It was a huge overstep, but I was curious. "I could have never afforded the house on my dog walking salary," she said. "So I bought a condo while I lived with my dad. He helped me renovate it. More like I helped him. I was going to move into it, but that was right around the time he got sick. I rented it out to cover the mortgage. That proved to be a pretty good deal. Another apartment close to the beach went on the market. My dad convinced me to buy it. He told me the real estate market was a solid investment. At the time, we thought there was a chance he might beat the cancer. I bought the apartment, and once again, we renovated it. He got sicker, and it was almost impossible for me to work at all."

"You took care of him," I said with admiration.

"Yes. The rentals pretty much paid for themselves. My dad passed away, and I had his house. I couldn't live in it. I sold it, made almost no money from the sale, and moved into the place I'm in now. My mother passed away a short time later. I got a small inheritance from her estate. I thought about paying off the bills, but I had been eyeing that property for about a month. I don't know why, but it appealed to me. Instead of paying off bills, I used it to put a down payment on the house. I used the rest of the money to replace appliances and pay for the initial repairs."

"You're very money savvy," I said. "That was smart."

"I don't have much to fall back on," she said. "The rentals are an investment in my future. If I get fired or one of my jobs goes under, I know I still have the rental stream. It would take an apocalypse to keep people from coming to Hawaii. I might have to lower the rent, but it will still pay the mortgage."

"Like I said, very savvy."

"Thank you." She grinned. "It was my dad's solid advice."

"Sounds like a smart man," I said.

"The smartest, kindest and most loyal man."

"So this was definitely worth the early morning wake-up call," I said. "This was well worth the tour guide fee."

"You're paying way too much," she said.

"Do any of your other guests get this level of service?" I asked.

"Definitely not," she replied. "But none of my other guests have offered to pay me to be their tour guide."

"Ah, I'm not special," I teased.

"You know you're very special," she said. "I have to get back, but I can come back this afternoon."

"I think this was definitely worth the money," I said. "Don't rush back. I can keep myself entertained."

We started back down the narrow path to the car. It was a hell of a way to start the day. On the way to the site, I had been thinking I was going to go back to the house and go right back to bed. Not now. I was ready to go for a long run on the beach. I wanted to breathe the fresh air.

"Thanks again," I said when she pulled to a stop. "It was, well I don't use this word often, but it was magnificent. It truly was the most beautiful scene. Better than a picture."

"I'm glad you enjoyed it," she said. "There are plenty of places just like that all around the island."

"I can't wait to see more."

I walked in the house and had to take a minute to sort through everything I was feeling in the moment. It was confusing. I couldn't tell if I was riding the high of the amazing scene or if it was being with her. Did I have feelings for her? That wasn't possible. I didn't really know her. I chalked it up to feeling free and enjoying the moment.

Chapter Fourteen

Ava

"You're smiling again," Cindy said.

I laughed and sprayed foam in the cup. "I can't help it."

"If I didn't know any better, I would say someone is falling for her renter," she said.

"No. Definitely not. It's just been a good week. I think I forgot just how beautiful this place we called home is. It's been exciting to see it through his eyes. I love that so much of it has remained a secret."

"Are you seeing him today?" she asked.

I nodded. "Yep."

"Girl, you've got it bad."

"No," I argued.

"Liar."

I didn't want to admit she was right. I knew it was stupid to fall for a man that was going to be leaving soon. I told myself it was just an innocent flirtation. It wasn't a relationship. We were spending time together and enjoying each other's company. He wanted to see the island, and I was happy to show it to him. He showed the proper enthusiasm and appreciation for all the places I showed him.

It made me appreciate the beauty of my home even more. I had taken him to my favorite restaurants. We'd gone to several waterfalls and down to the beach. Every day I went to the house to pick him up, he looked a little better. Not that he'd looked bad before, but he just looked healthier. He looked happier. He had not shaved all week. I was digging the scruff. It didn't look like he was doing his hair with a bunch of hair product either. I liked it.

At the end of my shift, I pulled off my apron and went to the break-room. Cindy was sitting down with her feet up. "Are you out of here?" she asked.

"I am," I said. "Did you need me for something else?"

"No, go play with your man," she teased.

"Stop. He's not my man. We're having fun together. And he's paying me to show him around. It's another job. A very well-paying job. If I don't show him a good time, I'm not earning my pay."

She gave me a dry look. "Is that really the line you're going to take? He's paying you to be this happy?"

"I'll admit, we do have fun together. We have been spending a few hours a day together, and it's been nice to hang out with someone other than my dog."

"I get it," she said. "I'm not blaming you for having a good time. I saw him. We all did. He's very attractive. He seems nice, and he's made you smile like we haven't seen in a long time."

"I am having fun with him, but I'm not fooling myself into thinking there will ever be anything between us," I assured her. "He leaves in a couple of weeks. I'm not doing the fling thing. It's just been nice to revisit places I haven't seen in a while. I don't have kids, but I think this is kind of what parents feel on Christmas morning or when they take their kids to Disneyland for the first time. I'm seeing things through his eyes. It's exciting."

"I understand," she said with a smile. "I'm just glad you're getting to do this. It's good for you. You're glowing. If you want to take a few days off, say the word. I'll get someone to cover your shifts. Spend time with him."

"No, no," I said. "I'm fine. I'm not going to disrupt my world. When he leaves, I'm still going to be here. I still have bills to pay."

"I understand," she said.

I left the shop and went home to change and get ready for the day out with Ethan. I was taking him surfing. I shoved my gear into the back seat and headed to his place. I knocked on the door and waited. He answered the door wearing a pair of swim trunks and a T-shirt.

"Are you ready for this?" I asked him.

"If I said no would that change your mind about putting my life in danger?" he countered.

"Stop," I laughed. "Your life will be just fine. I'm taking you to the baby waves. It's not like we're going to the North Shore."

"I would get laughed all the way back to New York," he said. "I'm prepared to eat sand, but I'm not interested in drowning."

"We'll just do a little introduction to surfing," I assured him. "Get you up on the board close to the shore. Do a little paddling and have fun."

He shook his head. "In all the years I've been to Hawaii and live right next to the ocean, I've never been interested in surfing."

"Liar," I teased. "When we were at the beach the other day, you were watching the surfers and envying them. If you don't like it, we'll stop."

"Do you know CPR?" he asked.

"Uh, yes, why?"

"I just want to make sure someone is close by to revive me," he said dryly.

I started laughing and couldn't stop. His dry sense of humor kept me on my toes. He had a tough exterior, but I saw the funny side. The softer side he was keeping hidden away. We got to the beach and rented two boards.

He pulled off his shirt and tossed it on the pile of our things. It actually took my breath away. He was cut. I had gotten a glimpse of him when I barged in on him in bed last week, but seeing all his skin and muscles in the bright light of day was an experience. I could see him on a stage stripping for a crowd of screaming women. I'd be right up at the front stuffing dollar bills in his underwear.

"Ready?" I said and cleared my throat.

"As I'll ever be," he replied.

I didn't miss him checking me out. My swimsuit was nothing explicit. Boy shorts and a sports bra type top. It was pretty standard. I didn't like my tits hanging out or the bottoms riding up. I walked down to the beach with him beside me.

"Let's go," I said when he stopped at the water's edge.

I walked into the water up to my knees and dropped my board into the water. He followed my lead. We spent the next hour trying to get him up on the board for more than three seconds. I was surprised by his lack of athleticism given his body.

We straddled our boards out in the water. The water rocked us back and forth. "I suck," he said.

"You don't suck," I assured him.

"No, I suck," he insisted. "I think there was a reason I've never tried this before. I firmly believe you cannot teach an old dog new tricks."

"You're not old," I said. "You did great that last run."

"Three seconds is not great," he said. "How long have you been surfing?"

"My parents had us out on the water very early," I told him. "I think I was four, maybe five the first time my dad put me on his surfboard. I'm not great at it. I just do it for fun."

"You're good," he said.

"Only compared to you," I teased. "Ready to try again?"

"I'm not sure ready is the correct term," he groaned.

We went through the process once again. A small wave rolled in, which I thought was perfect for him. "Go, go, go!" I encouraged.

He paddled out to the wave and got up on shaky legs. I hung back and watched. I wanted him to experience the high of riding through it. He stretched his arms out and rocked back and forth before catching his balance.

"Yes!" I screamed and clapped my hands. "Hold it! Pull through it!"

He started laughing and lost his balance, face-planting into the water. "Ethan!" I called out and quickly paddled over to where he had gone under. He shot back up and shook his head. "Are you okay?" I asked with concern.

"I'm fine," he said with a laugh. "That was rough."

I pushed his board toward him. He climbed on and wiped sand from his arm. "Are you sure you're okay?"

"I'm fine," he insisted. "But I need a drink."

"You deserve it," I said.

We paddled back to shore. He collapsed onto his stomach with his arms stretched out. "I'm alive. I feel like I should kiss the ground."

I shoved at his shoulder. "You're fine."

His skin was warm. I was so tempted to put my hand on his back. The few days we'd spent on the beach had tanned his skin. I opened the cooler and grabbed us each a soda. "Here," I said. "Rehydrate."

"I'm pretty sure I drank half the ocean," he muttered. He rolled to his side and went up on his elbow. I didn't know if he was doing it on purpose, but he looked like he was modeling. I had to force myself to look away. I sipped my drink and stared out at the water. I was having a serious crisis of conscience. I should not be lusting after the man. He was my renter. He was leaving. Getting mixed up was just going to leave me feeling bad.

"Which is why you need to drink something other than seawater," I said.

To distract myself, I checked my phone. There were two missed calls and a text. "Shit," I sighed.

"What's wrong?" he asked.

"One of my renters is having an issue with the kitchen sink," I said. "I don't want to be rude, but I need to call them back."

"Hey, don't mind me, I'll be here dying," he said.

I called the number of the renter. "Hi, this is Ava, I just got your message," I said as cheerily as possible. "What's going on?"

I listened to the person talk and cringed. "Can you put a bowl under the sink and I'll be there within the hour?"

I ended the call and looked over at Ethan in all his glory. "I'm sorry, I have to go."

"What's going on?" he asked.

"One of the rentals has something going on with the kitchen sink," I said. "I have to take care of it. I'll drop you off on the way."

"I'll go with you," he said. "If you don't want to take me all the way up to the house."

"You don't want to hang out with me while I fix a sink," I told him.

"It's not like I have anything to do," he said. "Besides, I want to see you in action."

I got up and started packing up our things. He pulled on his shirt. "You really don't have to do this," I told him.

"It's fine," he said again. "I don't mind. I'm just going to go back to the house and sit alone."

"Then I'd be happy to have an apprentice," I said.

I glanced over at him a couple of times. There was definitely something happening. I started to entertain the idea of a fling, but I quickly shut it down. I couldn't do it. I was not built for flings. I didn't have that gene, unfortunately. Sometimes, I thought things would be easier if I could just have a fling here and there. But I was looking for love.

Chapter Fifteen

Ethan

The apartment had a great view and was right on the beach, but it wasn't nearly as nice as the house. I got out of the car and looked around. She opened her trunk and pulled out an actual toolbox. "Really?" I asked with surprise.

"What?" She shrugged. "I have to be prepared. If a tenant calls, I have to make sure I fix whatever is broken. If not, I lose the rent and my reputation."

"I get it. I'm just having a hard time with you carrying a toolbox. I'm feeling very emasculated."

"Would you prefer to carry it?" she asked.

"Maybe," I laughed.

She pushed it toward me. I took it from her and shook my head. She was wearing her flip-flops, cutoff jean shorts, and a tank top over her bathing suit. I was going to have some serious wet dreams about her in that bathing suit. But seeing her carrying the toolbox was also pretty damn sexy.

She used her key to open the door. "Maintenance," she called out.

"They told me they were going to be gone," she said. "I just had to be sure."

The place was small but clean and looked to be in good repair. I noticed it had been recently updated. Ava went to the kitchen sink and groaned.

"What's wrong?" I asked.

"It's plugged," she sighed. "I'm guessing they put something down the drain. I thought they said it was leaking."

She opened the bottom cupboard. There was a bowl under the drain, but it was dry. I wasn't a plumber, but I was pretty certain it wasn't leaking. "Do you have that liquid stuff to unclog it?" I asked. I was trying to be helpful.

"No," she said. "I'll try the plunger."

She walked out of the kitchen and returned a few seconds later with a plunger. I stood back and watched her work.

"Shit," she muttered. "Things are about to get messy."

"How so?"

"I'm going to have to take apart the drain," she sighed. She took the toolbox and opened it up. I watched as she pulled out a couple of tools.

She knelt in front of the sink and started to work. "Do you know what you're doing?" I asked.

"Yes."

"Are you sure?" I asked with some concern.

"Yes," she laughed. "It's just a pipe."

I leaned back and watched her work. "Where did you learn how to fix a sink?" I asked.

"My dad," she said. "Like I said, he helped me renovate the first property. Then he supervised the next one. I can't do anything with the electrical stuff, but I can do a lot of it."

"If my sink stops up, I call a plumber," I said.

"Plumbers are expensive," she pointed out. "I can't afford to call a plumber to fix a plugged sink. I'm sure it's nothing. It'll be a quick fix. I can handle it."

"I guess I'm lucky I never had to learn how to do stuff like unclog a sink," I said.

"Lucky or unlucky," she said with her head under the sink, "I don't have to wait for someone to fix something for me."

I laughed and nodded. "True. But I bet you can't sit at the head of a conference table at a board meeting and answer questions about everything from payroll to a profit and loss report."

She popped her head up. "You'd lose that bet," she said with a grin. "Trust me, I very much can sit in a board meeting and answer questions. I just choose not to."

"Have you?"

"I've been involved in those meetings before," she said.

I believed her. She was a Jill of all trades. I admired her a little more every day. I learned something new about her every time we were together. She was young but had lived a lot. I admired her ability to just keep going. I found myself truly interested in getting to know her better.

"Can you hand me that pipe wrench?" she asked.

I stared into the toolbox. "Want to tell me what color that would be?"

She laughed. "It has a blue handle."

I spotted it and handed it to her.

"Thanks," she said. "Dammit!"

"What's wrong?" I asked.

"I see the leak," she groaned. "I knew I was going to have to replace this fitting. I hope I can fix it until the renters are gone."

"Is it clogged or leaking?"

"Both," she answered.

There was a sudden gush of water. "Are you okay?" I asked and squatted low to see what was happening.

"Yes, just cleared the leak," she replied. I watched her work. She put the pipe back together and then slid out from under the sink. "I need to shut off the main water supply so I can try and fix that leak."

"Is there something I can do to help?" I asked. "I feel useless, like a bump on a log."

"You're not a bump on a log." She smiled. "This shouldn't take me long. I'm sorry."

"Don't be sorry," I said. "I'm learning something new."

I followed her down the hall. She was very capable. She turned off a water valve and went back to the kitchen. "This is where it gets dicey," she said.

"How so?"

"Because I have yet to do this without getting sprayed with water," she replied. "It always goes badly."

She grabbed another tool and went back under the sink. I had never felt more useless in my life. "Do you have to do these kinds of repairs a lot?" I asked.

"I wouldn't say a lot, but more than zero," she replied. "The house you're in required a lot of plumbing. Let's hope this goes better than that."

"Yes, let's hope."

I watched her under the sink. "Dammit!" she cursed and threw a towel.

"What's wrong?"

"I cannot get this fitting loosened," she said.

"I could try," I offered.

She popped her head out. "Are you sure? I feel terrible for having my renter fix another property."

"I think I'm a little more than just a renter."

She handed me a tool. "I'll show you."

We both managed to wedge ourselves under the sink. She pointed me to the fitting she was struggling with. I wrenched on it until it was loose. "I've never felt more like a man than in this moment," I said with a laugh.

"Glad I could elevate your ego," she said.

I slid out from under the sink and watched while she put some white tape around a pipe. She went back under the sink and started working again. "Okay," she said. "I think I got it. Do you want to use those big manly muscles and tighten it up for me?"

"When you put it like that, how could I say no?"

I dropped back down and tightened it down. "I'm going to turn on the water," she said. "Let me know if it leaks."

I stayed under the sink and waited to tell her we had fixed it. Unfortunately, that was not what happened. There was a noise followed by water spraying me in the face. "Ava!" I called out. "Ava, no!"

"What's wrong?" she asked and rushed into the kitchen. I had my hand over the spraying pipe like that would somehow stop it. It didn't.

"Not fixed!" I shouted.

"Oh shit!" She rushed away, and a few seconds later the water stopped.

I slipped out from under the sink with water dripping from my face. Ava came back into the kitchen, took one look at me, and started laughing. "Oh no," she said. "Are you okay?"

"I'm fine. I'm wet."

"Did you see where the water was coming from?" she asked and dropped to her knees.

"Everywhere," I replied.

"Was it the same pipe?"

"Yes," I said.

She stuck her head under the sink and cursed. "I don't think I had it on right. I'll put on more tape. If I can't get it fixed, I'm going to have to go to the hardware store and get a whole new pipe."

"Put more of that stuff on there." I pointed at the stretchy tape. "Then I'll tighten it down."

"Second time's a charm," she teased.

"I certainly hope so," I muttered and grabbed the dish towel from the stove. I wiped my face. "I guess it's a good thing I'm still in my swim trunks."

"I really am sorry," she said. "I didn't think that would happen."

"Me either," I said. "Let me do it."

I took the wrench and replaced the pipe. I made sure it was all the way on and then tightened it down. I gave it a good jiggle, convinced we had it right.

"Do I dare?" she asked.

"Go for it," I said. "The worse that can happen is I get wet again, right?"

She nodded.

This time, I waited for the water to come on without my face being under the sink.

"Ready?" she called out.

"Do it!"

I waited to be sprayed with water. When it didn't happen, I got up and did a little victory dance. "It worked!"

She came into the kitchen and smiled. "Now comes the real test."

"What would that be?" I asked wearily.

"Now we turn on the water and see if we have a blowout," she said with a grimace.

She turned on the faucet, and we both waited. The water trickled out and went down the drain. She turned the faucet up higher before bending down to look under the sink. She gave a thumbs up. "It looks like it's working."

"Thank God," I muttered.

"I'll clean up, and we'll go," she said. "Thank you for your help."

"It was interesting," I said. "I can honestly say I've done something new today. I might even be brave enough to try and fix my own sink."

"Let's not get carried away," she said. "You saw what an experienced plumber can do."

"Are you calling yourself an experienced plumber?" I asked.

"More experienced than the other person in this room."

"Fair enough." I nodded.

"I think it will hold," she said. "I was going to wrap it, but I don't think I need to. I'll just come back later and fix it right. Hopefully, they don't pour grease down the damn sink again."

She knelt down and dropped her tools back into the box. I watched her work. This was the sexy plumber in porn movies except the roles were reversed. All she needed was a tool belt slung around her hips. When she stood, we were facing each other. She reached up and pushed some of the wet hair from my forehead. "You're soaked."

"I'll dry." My voice was hoarse. Standing close to her was doing something to me. My eyes dropped to her mouth. It would be so easy to kiss her. I was pretty sure she would let me do it. She'd kiss me back. All day we had been doing this dance. Ever since she'd stripped out of those shorts, I had been thinking about sex. Not just sex, but sex with her. I wanted her. I found myself bargaining with someone, but I didn't know who. My conscience? If I allowed myself just one kiss, it would satisfy my craving.

Chapter Sixteen

Ava

Kissing him would be bad. He was my renter. Kissing him just once would be like eating just one chip. I had a feeling there was no such thing as one kiss when it came to him. He had the mouth of a man that could kiss very well.

The sexual tension that had been burning just under the surface all day was very real. Standing this close to him made me very aware of that chemistry. I was still feeling the tingling from seeing him on the beach. I had been trying to fight the feelings all day.

I licked my lips. He sucked in a breath. His eyes met mine. I knew what happened next. I had a moment of clarity. I could turn and walk away or stay right where I was and wait for it. I wasn't about to move. He grabbed me around the waist and pushed me up against the counter with his forehead touching mine. His breath washed over me. I could feel him trying to figure out what do next. He had the same reservations. We had never explicitly said we weren't going to hook up. It was more of an unspoken understanding.

I dropped my eyes to his mouth. He got the meaning. His mouth covered mine in a flash. I gasped, sucking his tongue into my mouth. He didn't hold back. His tongue slashed across mine. His hips pinned me between his body and the unmoving counter pushing into my ass. His hands slid under my shirt and over my flesh. Goosebumps spread over my flesh. He grabbed my breast through the thin bathing suit top. My nipples hardened immediately. A moan escaped my throat.

He moved his hips, lowering his body and giving me a taste of what he had to offer. I ran my hands through his hair like I had been longing to do since I'd first laid eyes on him. I pulled his head closer to mine with his hands massaging my breasts. He kissed me with a hunger that matched my own.

The door opened with laughter followed by "Oh!"

I pushed him off me. He kept his back to the intruders. "Hi, uh, sink's fixed!"

The couple looked at me with surprise, amusement, and maybe even a hint of disgust. "You're the landlord?" the woman asked.

"Yes. I fixed the sink. It was clogged as well. I fixed that. We'll be going. Feel free to call if you need anything else. Ethan, we should go."

He reached down and grabbed the toolbox. I noticed he was carrying it in front of him. I knew what he was hiding. I had felt it pushing against me seconds ago. I made a beeline for the door with him hot on my heels. We rushed back to my car. He put the toolbox in the trunk while I waited in the driver's seat.

I knew my face was eight shades of red. I was humiliated. Absolutely mortified. We'd been making out like teenagers whose parents were gone for the weekend. And subsequently busted. I hoped it didn't completely ruin my reputation. I would send over a food basket and apologize for messing around in the kitchen. I didn't want them to think I snuck into my rental properties and fucked around while the tenants were away.

I didn't even ask if he was ready to go home. I had to drop him off. I could not spend another ten minutes with him. I knew what would happen if I did. The sexual tension between us we thick and heavy. I could feel it hanging there. Neither of us said a word as I drove. I was certain he was having the same regrets. We'd let the moment get away from us. We both knew better.

"Do you want to come in?" he asked when I stopped in the driveway.

"No." I realized that was a little harsh. "I mean, I can't. I need to go get some parts, and I've got to let Roxy out."

"Will I see you tomorrow?" he asked.

"I have to work at four," I said without looking at him. "In the morning. Maybe in the afternoon."

"Okay." He nodded. "Thanks for the surf lesson."

"Anytime," I said.

The moment he was out of the car, I sped away. I needed to put some distance between us. I blew out a breath. That had been stupid. We'd had a lot of fun together, but I could not fall for a man that was going to leave soon. I didn't need a broken heart.

I got home and let Roxy out. I took a quick shower with thoughts of him still weighing me down. I was stretched out on the couch when my phone started ringing. My first thought was Ethan. Was he calling to tell me he no longer wanted my tour guide services? I wouldn't blame him. I glanced at the screen and saw the name.

I immediately snatched my phone. "You're alive!" I answered with a laugh. "How was it?"

"It was amazing," my best friend Andrea answered. "We got back yesterday."

"I saw your pictures on Insta. It was like being there with you."

"Liar," she laughed. "I wish I could share the bug bites with you."

She'd been essentially backpacking across Europe for the last three months. I envied her as far as getting to see the world, but I didn't envy the nomadic experience. I liked the roots I'd put down. I could never stay gone for months at a time.

"Are you in LA?" I asked.

"Yep, and I'm not going anywhere for a long time," she said. "I think I got the wandering spirit out of my system. It was amazing, but I'm over it."

"Your parents will be happy to have you home," I said.

"Tell me what you've been up to," she said. "Did you get the new house all done?"

"I did," I answered. "It's done. Well, not done, but it's officially rented."

"Woohoo!"

"It has been a huge weight off my shoulders," I said. "I want to keep working on it, but for now, I can rent it as is."

"Good for you," she said. "Anything on the man front?"

I immediately thought of Ethan. He wasn't my man, but there was definitely something budding. Andrea and I had met in the eighth grade and been best friends ever since. Our lives had gone in very different directions, but she understood why I'd left my mother's family to forge my own path. She was still in that life, living off her family's money and not worried about a job or anything else.

"So it's pretty weird you called," I said. "I was just sitting here kicking myself in the ass."

"Why?"

"I just made out with the guy renting my house," I blurted out.

"Wow. Is that a perk? Is there a box someone checks to get that perk?"

"Very funny," I sighed. "If you saw this guy, you would understand the temptation."

"He's hot?"

"Very," I said. "Crazy hot. When I first met him, I was not impressed. I mean, I knew he was hot, but his attitude sucked. He's wealthy and arrogant. He needed help, and I took pity on him. Turns out, he isn't so bad. He offered to pay me to be his tour guide. The last week, we've been spending time together."

"How old is this guy?" she asked.

"Thirty-seven." I sighed. "There's been this sexual tension burning between us. I don't want to do anything about it because he leaves in a couple of weeks."

"That's perfect!" she exclaimed. "A hot guy with no strings is perfect."

"Not for me," I said. "I don't want a fling. I don't even want a boyfriend. I like my life. I think I made myself believe nothing would happen. I didn't mind checking him out. It was fun and flirty. I didn't mind him checking me out, but I never really thought it would go anywhere."

"And you just made out?" she asked.

"Yes. I'm so confused. I'm still crazy about him, but I can't."

"You're trying to talk yourself out of sex?" she scoffed. "Girl, you're crazy. Take yourself to the store and get some condoms. Then you go find him and use the whole damn box."

"Stop!"

"I'm serious," she laughed. "When is the last time you had sex? Gone on a date for that matter?"

"A long time. I've had shitty luck in the relationship department, you know that. It's such a pain in the ass. I love my freedom. I love going to bed at seven o'clock on a Friday and no one is going to say shit about it. I can do what I want. I don't want the trappings of a relationship. It's not worked out well for me."

"You don't have to marry the guy," she said. "But you're stopping yourself from having a good time because you think it might not end well."

"It's not like I'm looking at him as a potential husband or even a boyfriend, but you know me," I said. "I don't have that shutoff switch like you and everyone else. I go to bed with a guy, and I get my heart all mixed up in things."

"Because you're a sweetheart," she said with a smile in her voice. "It's why I love you. Maybe don't take him to bed. That doesn't mean you can't have a little fun."

"It's just weird," I said. "I don't really know much about him. He might have a crazy ex-wife at home. He might have a serious girlfriend. He's here by himself, and it's pretty clear he's running from something. I know he's having a hard time with his family right now, but that's all I know. I don't want to get into the middle of a messy whatever he's got going on."

"How did it end?" she asked.

"How did what end?"

"The make-out session," she said. "Did he stop it? Did you?"

"Uh, well, it ended when the tenants renting the apartment we were in came through the front door," I said with the embarrassment flooding back.

"No!" Her laughter echoed through the phone. "Why would you go to the apartment? You have your place, the house, what in the world?"

"It was a weird moment," I sighed. "I had to fix the sink. He got sprayed with water, and one thing just led to another. We only kissed for a few minutes before they came in. Just long enough for him to get hard and have his hand up my shirt."

She was still laughing. "You get yourself into the weirdest situations."

"I know," I groaned. "Those renters must think I'm a freak. We were in the kitchen. They saw us kissing. I know they noticed him trying to hide what he was packing."

"Speaking of," she cooed. "Was it something you'd like to work with?"

"Stop."

"It was!" She laughed again.

"You're a terrible influence on me," I muttered.

"I told you that from the first day we met," she said. "You knew the risks when you became my friend."

"I don't know what I'm going to do," I said. "I should leave him alone."

"I vote you have fun with him," she said.

"I know your opinion," I sighed. "I don't know what to do. I have to work in the morning. I'll wait and see if he calls. If he doesn't, I'll take that as he needs to put some distance between us. If you saw this guy, you would understand what I meant when I said he's hot. He's the kind of guy that would date the hottest women in the world. I'm not in his league. I don't think I want to be in his league."

"Again, you don't have to marry the guy," she said. "Just have some fun. You work so hard. All work and no play makes Ava a very dull girl. A very dull, unsatisfied girl. You know you miss sex."

"It's not about the sex," I said. "All work and no play means I don't have time to miss sex."

"That's probably why you're so hot for him," she said. "Don't beat yourself up for wanting a guy. It's natural."

"Thanks," I said. "I've missed you."

"I'm back now. I don't plan on going anywhere for a long while. Call me anytime."

"I will," I said. "Get some rest and recover."

After hanging up with her, I felt better. I wasn't going to overthink it. It was a kiss. A few kisses. I would take a few days off from the tour guide role. We'd let things cool down. Hopefully, we could just go back to flirting without it going any further than that.

Chapter Seventeen

Ethan

I woke without an alarm. It was quickly becoming my routine. I could get very used to a life without ten meetings packed into a day. I liked going for my morning run and then enjoying a leisurely cup of coffee on the deck. I had taken Ava's advice and left my phone off most of the time. If it wasn't off, I left it in the other room. I didn't need to check it twenty times.

I tied my shoes and headed out the front door. I didn't even have to take keys with me. I didn't need to lock the door. That was definitely not like New York. I jogged down to the beach and went my usual route. While I ran, I thought about what I was going to do for the day. I was pretty sure I wasn't going to see Ava. She had practically run away from me yesterday.

The kiss might have been a mistake, but I didn't think she was pissed about it. She'd certainly been enjoying the moment. I could not explain what made me kiss her. She was standing there look sexy as hell, and the urge was stronger than my self-control. I knew she'd been thinking about kissing me. I saw her look at my mouth. She had wanted me to kiss her.

It wasn't the kiss; it was the location. My timing could have been better. We had spent hours alone, and I'd never kissed her. The one time we weren't in a good place, I kissed her. I could still feel her lips on mine. She was a damn good kisser. And her boobs. Damn, they were perfect. Not too big, not too small, just perfect.

That might have been my one and only chance to touch those beautiful boobs. She'd made it clear she didn't want anything to do with me once we got in the car. The silence on the way home had been awkward. I wasn't even sure what I was supposed to say. I didn't want to apologize. That would make it seem like I regretted it, and I definitely didn't. I did regret making her feel like she couldn't be around me without me trying to mount her.

I finished my jog and flopped onto the sand. The sun beat down on me. I loved that I didn't have to rush back. I didn't have to rush anywhere. I was lying on a beach with the sand on my skin and very few cares. It was the first time in a long time I'd felt so free. My phone was back at the house, and I wasn't freaking out.

This was what I had been longing for. I didn't even know I was missing out on moments like this one. I had spent the last fifteen years busting my ass and ignoring the fact that life was passing me by. I wasn't living. I was working. I was going through the motions. I woke up every morning to nonstop messages and demands on my time. I went to the office and dealt with one problem after another until it was time to go home and go to bed. That was not a life. I had plenty of money, but it didn't make a bit of difference if I couldn't enjoy it. I was going to go to my grave with a pile of money in the bank and no one to mourn me.

I had to make a change. I knew it, but every day I was here, it only confirmed it further. After enjoying the lazy morning, I got up and started the walk back to the house. I was disappointed I wouldn't get to see Ava today, but I told myself to let it go. I could hang out and relax.

I went straight for the shower without checking my phone. I dressed and made my coffee. My phone started vibrating, and I looked at the screen. It was my brother. I declined the call. The voicemail icon was on. As much as I didn't want to know, I kind of had to. Being the CEO saddled with me some responsibilities. I couldn't completely shirk them.

I called into voicemail, put it on speaker, and searched for something to eat.

"Ethan." My mother sounded exasperated. "What is going on? I don't understand why you're not calling me back. This isn't like you. I'm worried about you. I am guessing you are trying to hide. That's not the right way to handle this. We need you to come home. There are some serious issues that we have to deal with. There is a reporter sniffing around. This story is going to break soon. This is serious, Ethan. Call me."

I deleted the message and let the next one play. "Ethan, man, where the hell are you?" Collin asked. "I'm fucked. I need my big brother back here. Shit is heating up fast. Mom and Dad are freaking out. Dad is calling in favors, but this thing isn't going away. You've got to come back. I don't know why you're hiding. It's my ass on the line. This is making you look guilty, and your guilt is going to rub off on me. No one will fuck with us if we stick together. Call me. Seriously, this is real."

I deleted the message, muttering, "You're in trouble, dickhead, not me."

I was so sick of pulling the weight for the whole family. Collin did whatever he wanted and never worried about the consequences. He lived his life without a care in the world. Only now that he was trying to climb up the political ladder did he start thinking about his choices. That wasn't true. He was still being reckless, but now the stakes were higher. He just assumed everyone was going to jump in and save him because he was important. Fuck everyone else and what it might cost them. As long as he had a good time, that's all he thought about.

It pissed me off that my parents were still bailing him out. He was thirty-two. They coddled him and expected me to jump and save him at every turn. I was supposed to be the good one, and it was just kind of accepted that Collin would fuck off. I wondered what they thought was going to happen when they were gone. Did they expect me to save his ass? I didn't think I could do it. His latest fuck-up was extremely serious. Someone had lost their life. That was not a burden I wanted to carry. It was on him. He could not keep playing with people's lives.

There were a couple more messages from my assistant and then my mother. I deleted them without listening. They were killing my vibe. I took my coffee out to the deck and left my phone inside. I realized I was trying to put distance between us any way I could. I couldn't deal with them.

I stared out at the lush green landscape of the backyard. Everywhere I looked, it was green. I had spent so much of my life in the concrete jungle that was New York. I rarely took time off. When I did take the time to go out to the Hamptons, I was still working. I was always working.

I thought about what I dreamed about doing when I was chained to my desk. Then it came to me. I knew what I was going to do. I hopped up and grabbed my phone. I did a quick search and then made a call. Sometimes, it was good to have money in the bank. I changed again and grabbed the keys to head out. I went by the coffee shop first only to find out Ava had already worked and gone home for the day.

I drove to her apartment and knocked on the door. I assumed she was home. Her car was in the driveway. I waited and then knocked again. Was she actually going to pretend she wasn't home? That was fucked up. She did not need to hide from me. I was about to walk away when she opened the door.

"Ethan?"

"Were you asleep?" I asked.

"I was just taking a quick nap. It was an early morning, and I didn't get much sleep last night."

"Oh, do you have to work this afternoon?" I asked. "The dogs?"

"No." She shook her head.

"Great. Did you get enough sleep?"

"Yes, why?" she asked suspiciously.

"Why don't you get dressed?" I said. "It's my turn to take you out."

"Take me out?" she questioned.

"Yes." I nodded. "Something casual."

She opened her door and gestured for me to go in. Roxy was dead asleep on the couch. "Some watchdog," I joked.

"She's definitely not a watchdog." Ava smirked. "But I don't really need her to be. She's just my buddy."

I was trying to keep my distance. I didn't want to crowd her and make her uncomfortable. I got the distinct feeling she wanted space. I wasn't willing to walk away from her, from the friendship we had formed. She was important to me. I didn't know if I would ever talk to her again after I left Oahu, but for now, I didn't want to ruin what we had.

"Are you going to get dressed?" I asked, trying not to look at her. It was a very conscious effort to keep my eyes on hers. She was wearing tiny little shorts and a tank top that hugged her body. I'd had my hands on those perfect tits yesterday, and it was hard not to look at them. Not to fantasize about touching them.

"What do you have up your sleeve?" she asked.

"I don't plan on throwing you into the ocean," I said with a laugh. "Trust me. I've trusted you all week. It's my turn. My turn to show you a good time."

"Okay." She shrugged. "Give me a minute."

"I'll be here with Roxy," I said. I moved to sit on the couch next to the dog, which had still not moved. She was a very chill animal. I found myself looking at the picture of Ava's dad on the wall once again. He looked like a fun guy. I would have liked to have met him.

I absently scratched behind Roxy's ears. "You don't mind me stealing your mom, right? I would take you, but I'm not sure this is the right adventure for you. Maybe next time."

I hoped Ava was cool with this. I wasn't good at just letting things happen. I was used to driving the bus and making them happen. I didn't sit on the bench. When I saw something I wanted, I went after it. I was not going to sit back and let the kiss destroy the friendship. I wasn't going to let her hide. If she didn't want to have anything to do with me, she was going to have to say it. Then, and only then, would I give her what she wanted.

Chapter Eighteen

Ava

I pulled on a pair of shorts. He wasn't telling me where we were going. That excited and worried me. I liked that he wasn't bringing up the kiss. If we could just pretend it never happened, that would be great. I pulled my hair into a ponytail. I wasn't really worried he was going to do anything. He had trusted me. I could trust him.

When I returned to the living room, he was sitting on the couch with Roxy. How could I not trust the guy that had won over my dog? Roxy was a good judge of character. If she liked him, he had to be a decent man.

"All right," I said. "I'm ready."

It didn't take long before I figured out we were headed to the harbor. "What are we doing?" I asked.

"It's a surprise." He smiled.

I let him have his moment. He pointed to a sailboat at the end of the dock. "That's our ride."

"You rented a sailboat?" I asked. I knew how much that cost. Then I reminded myself he could afford it.

"I did." He nodded.

"Do you know how to sail?" I asked. I wasn't trying to get killed because some city boy had some idea sailing was easy.

"I do," he said. He stepped onto the boat and extended a hand to help me on.

"Because you've seen it on TV or you actually know?"

He laughed and moved around the boat, checking things out. "My family has a summer house in the Hamptons. We spent our summers sailing. I haven't done it in a couple of years, but I think I remember the basics."

I wasn't surprised by his Hamptons story. Of course, he would summer in The Hamptons. I sometimes forgot he was rich. He had changed since our first encounter. He was far more relaxed and more like the kind of people I hung around.

"If you forget, I know how to sail," I said. "Not well, but I know the basics."

"Between the two of us, we should be able to figure it out." He grinned. "I saw the picture at your house. You and your dad sailed?"

"My dad sailed," I laughed. "I was more of the pain in the ass getting in the way."

"I doubt that," he said. "I'm sure he taught you a lot."

I almost got emotional. "He did. It's crazy to think he taught me more in a few years then my mom and her family taught me in ten."

We worked together to get the boat out of the harbor. The day was perfect for sailing. He manned the wheel while I took a seat and let the wind blow through my hair. The whole experience was very emotional. Being on the water reminded me so much of my father. I missed him with my whole heart.

"Hey, what do you think about this spot?" Ethan asked.

"What about it?"

"I was going to drop anchor," he said.

I looked toward the shore, which was a distant line on the horizon. There were other boats on the water, but everyone kept a respectable distance. "I think here is perfect."

He set the anchor and went downstairs. I turned my face up to the sky and closed my eyes. The moment was perfect. I heard footsteps on the stairs and opened my eyes. Ethan held up a picnic basket.

"What is that?" I asked.

"Lunch."

"When did you have the time to do that?" I asked with a laugh.

"I didn't," he said. "I called someone and had it delivered to the boat. Ready to see what they chose for our picnic?"

"This should be interesting," I said.

He put the basket between us. There was a container of mac salad, sandwiches, and fresh fruit. Dessert was a small chocolate cake.

"What do you think?" he asked.

"I think it looks amazing, and I just realized I'm really hungry," I said.

We unwrapped our sandwiches. "This was really thoughtful," I said. "Thank you so much for bringing me out here. It's been too long since I've been on the water."

"Me too," he agreed. "I've been talking about going sailing for a long time. I thought that would be the first thing I did."

"How come you didn't?" I asked.

"I don't know," he sighed. "I guess I didn't want to do it alone. Thanks for coming with me."

"You're welcome," I replied.

We ate until we were both full. "I think I want to stretch out and soak up the sun," I told him.

"This thing turns into a bed," he said and got up from the sofa.

I helped him pull out the bottom and arranged the cushions. We both climbed onto it and stretched out. We didn't talk for several minutes. We just rocked and bobbed with the waves.

"I'm sorry I tripped out yesterday," I said.

"I'm sorry if I overstepped the boundaries," he replied. "I'm like a bull in a china shop when it comes to women. I guess there's a reason why I'm single. Perpetually single."

"I think that's something I was worried about," I said. "You're this way with everything. I don't believe you're single."

He laughed. "I assure you, I'm very single."

"Is there an ex?" I pressed.

"No," he said. "I'm serious when I say I'm a workaholic. I've dated but failed. I'm difficult to be with. I know that. I accept it. What about you?"

"Am I with someone?" I clarified.

"Yes, now or is there an ex waiting in the wings to swoop in and win you back?" he asked.

I shook my head. "No ex. I think my last boyfriend was in college. I have a hard time being tied down. My friend is always telling me I need to date more. My dad understood me. He understood my desire to be free. I love being independent. I have dated on occasion, but I always have this moment of sheer panic. I do a fast-forward into the future and see myself being miserable. Then it's just over. I haven't dated in a while. My friend Andrea thinks I'm a freak of nature."

"Why?"

"Because I'm not sad that I'm single," I laughed. "She thinks life should be about dating and seeing as many people as possible. I only wish I had her energy."

"No shit," he said with a laugh. "My brother is like that. He dates enough for both of us. Hell, he dates enough for an entire football team."

"Ah, a womanizer," I said.

"Something like that," he muttered.

"I think there is something to be said for people that can be comfortable and happy without being attached," I said. "At least that's what I'm going to hold on to. I think one day it will hit me, but I'm just not there."

"Agreed."

We fell into comfortable silence once again. This was the kind of thing I wanted in a relationship. I wanted to be able to just be. That was one of the things I hated most about relationships. There was all these games and the need to constantly try to impress the other person. I hated the song and dance. I hated that people thought they had to always be perfect.

I let out a long sigh. I was completely content with him. The ocean bobbed us up and down. I felt like we were being rocked to sleep. The sound of the water lapping against the side of the boat combined with the sun overhead was soothing. It was funny, but out on the water, it was easy to forget there were other people in the world. Everything faded. It was as if we had drifted away from all of life's troubles.

I felt him move beside me and opened my eyes. He was on his side with his head propped up on his elbow. He pushed up his sunglasses and looked down at me. I reached up and took off my own sunglasses. I wanted to be able to look into his eyes. The look I saw was the same one I had seen in the kitchen yesterday.

I knew I should tell him we couldn't. He would stop. He would lie back down, and we could enjoy the rest of our day. But the kiss yesterday had been so damn good. Andrea's words echoed through my head. It was just a kiss. Maybe more. It wasn't so bad. His hand reached up and brushed the hair from my shoulders. His light touch sent shivers down my spine. The voice telling me not to do it, not to kiss him or touch him faded. The voice of lust roared loud and clear. It was telling me to do it. Demanding I take the pleasure Ethan offered.

I put my hand on the side of his face, essentially giving him a bright green light. He leaned down and kissed me. It was a brush of his lips over mine. His butterfly kiss relaxed me even further, if that was possible. His hand caressed my bare arm. The kiss intensified. My hand slid into his hair and tugged at the back of his head to bring him closer.

He slipped his hand under my shirt and grabbed one breast. I moaned, giving in to the pleasure. His tongue dueled with mine. What started out slow and sweet quickly turned into fire. His body pressed against mine. I clawed at his back, tugging his shirt up. He pulled away and jerked his shirt over his head, dropping it to the floor. My hands spread out against his chest, massaging over the muscles. His mouth returned to mine at the same time he pulled at my shirt. Once again, he broke away and pushed my shirt up and over my head.

I sat up and grabbed his face to kiss him once again. His hands rubbed up and down my arms with a fervor that burned deep inside me. My hands roamed over his chest. I had been dying to get my hands on him since I saw him shirtless on the beach. To actually be able to touch him was thrilling. My head was spinning. I wanted him.

Things were moving fast. It was days of pent-up lust coming to a head. There was no stopping it. He pushed me back down and climbed over me. I welcomed him against me by wrapping one leg around his and pulling him close.

A noise that did not belong made us both freeze. "Shit," he murmured.

It was another boat. We were alone, but not that alone. A passing boat would get an eyeful. I laughed nervously. "Oops."

He rolled off me and grabbed my hand. "Downstairs," he murmured.

It was another chance to stop things. I didn't stop it. I fucking encouraged it. I hopped off the bed and let him lead me downstairs to the single room below. Once we were through the door, the clothes hit the floor in a flurry. I practically launched myself at him. Our naked bodies slammed together and fell to the bed. He climbed over me, kissing me until I was certain I was going to explode in a million little pieces.

"I've thought about this for days," he growled against my ear.

"Me too," I replied.

He stretched his naked body beside mine with his hand pressed against my belly. "You nearly killed me yesterday."

"How so?" I asked. I was barely able to form clear words. My head was cloudy. He was trailing his fingers over my stomach and breasts. My body was primed and ready. I wanted it. I wanted him.

"I couldn't stop thinking about you naked," he murmured before sucking my nipple into his mouth.

I nearly bucked him right off the bed. He sucked harder with his hand trailing down my stomach and moving between my legs. I willingly opened my legs to him. His fingers teased over my core before pushing one inside. I cried out again.

"I knew it," he said and moved his mouth to my other breast. "I knew you'd be wet and ripe and fucking perfect."

I was quickly spinning out, losing all control. My body was his to play and manipulate any way he wanted. I clawed at him and tried to pull him over me. The orgasm he brought me to was sweet and powerful and hit every inch of my body. I tingled from tip to top in the best way.

"Hold on," he said and rolled away.

I watched his naked ass stroll into the bathroom while it felt like I was floating. He returned a second later with a condom in his hand. I wasn't even bothered that he'd come prepared. I was glad he did. He quickly rolled it down his very large cock and rejoined me on the bed. He moved over the top of me, nudging my legs open. He pushed inside me, slow and sure until he was seated deep inside me.

My arms went around him and held his warm body close to mine. I could feel his heart pounding in his chest. I felt the same way. I held him tightly, appreciating every little spasm that rippled through me. Every spasm caused him to jerk, and his pulsating erection dragged out the after effects of the orgasm he had given me. Spasm after spasm rolled through me. I knew it would be good with him. I had known it and been a little afraid of it because it was going to be one of those things I was going to have a hard time living without.

Chapter Nineteen

Ethan

"I have to move," I grunted.

I had tried to hold back, but her tight pussy was squeezing and milking me. My hips were jerking of their own accord. Primal instinct was winning the battle. I could not stop it. I pushed myself up on my arms and thrust once.

Her sweet cry of pleasure had me doing it again and again. I thrust my hips over and over. Our bodies slapped together, the sounds alternating between grunts and moans to sharp little cries of pleasure. I wanted to drag out the moment forever. My body had other ideas. It was a little embarrassing to be on the verge of climax so quickly. I was chalking it up to the dry spell I'd been in and her. She was fucking amazing in every way. I connected with her like I had never connected with another human.

"I can't stop," I said through gritted teeth.

"Give it to me," she gasped. "Harder."

I shouted at the ceiling. The sound came from deep inside me. In my mind, I was racing toward a finish line. I was so close. I was going to scream across it. I sucked in a breath and then exploded. I was certain I blacked out. There were stars bursting behind my eyelids as I collapsed on top of her, sucking in deep breaths and trying to regain full consciousness. She had literally blown my mind.

"Fuck me," I breathed. "Holy shit."

She kissed the side of my cheek and patted my back. I didn't want to move. I would buy the damn boat. I didn't want to go back. If I could just stay right where I was for the rest of my days, I would die a happy man.

She had other ideas. She gently pushed at me until I moved off her. To my surprise and disappointment, she slid off the bed and collected her things before rushing into the bathroom. I didn't take her for a shy woman. Five minutes ago, she'd been sprawled naked beneath me. There had not been a hint of hesitation on her part.

She came out of the bathroom half-dressed. "I'm going to find my shirt," she said. "We should probably get back to shore."

"I have the boat for a couple more hours," I replied.

"I've got to do laundry," she said.

I wasn't sure if that was a step above or below the excuse about washing one's hair. "Okay," I said.

I doubted she heard me. She was climbing the stairs pretty damn fast. I took a minute to replay the last thirty minutes. I'd had the best sex of my life, and she couldn't get away from me fast enough. It wasn't exactly a compliment. I didn't understand what went wrong. She had been into it. I didn't pressure her into anything.

I climbed off the bed and went into the bathroom to clean up. I was drawn to the woman. Sex with her was unlike anything else I'd ever experienced. It wasn't just the physical pleasure. I really, really liked her. I felt like I could talk to her. She was down to earth and not all about money and power. They said opposites attract, and I believed it. But the more time I spent in Hawaii away from all the bullshit back in New York, I was beginning to think I might not be so different than she was. I could feel the real me clawing through the bullshit I'd been forced to accept. Maybe I was a guy that just needed the beach and a good woman at his side. None of the other stuff mattered.

I pulled on my shorts and made my way up top. She was already pulling up the anchor. She couldn't get away from me fast enough, apparently. I took over at the wheel while she cleaned up the picnic. It was pretty clear she was doing her best not to look at me. She was avoiding me the best she could while still being trapped on the boat with me.

I was kicking myself for crossing the line, but I'd really thought things were good. I'd thought she was into it. The last thing I wanted to do was ruin whatever had been budding between us. Apologizing felt wrong. I wasn't sorry we had sex. There was no way I could apologize for something that had felt that good.

Once in the car and on the way back to her house, the iciness between us only intensified. I pulled to a stop in front of her apartment with the intention of walking her inside. "Don't," she said when I cut the engine.

"What?"

"You don't need to walk me to the door," she said. "I won't be inviting you in."

It was a slap across the face. "Okay."

"I think you know your way around well enough," she said. "If there is something specific you want to see or do, you should probably find someone else to show you. I think it's best if I'm just your landlord."

I was stunned. She had turned off. All the way off. She opened the door to get out. I was not about to just let her walk away. "Ava, wait."

"Goodbye, Ethan."

She was out of the car in a flash. I threw open my door and stood to talk to her over the car. "Ava, stop."

She stopped and turned back to look at me. "What?"

"What is wrong? I don't understand. If you didn't want to have sex with me, a simple no would have sufficed. We were getting along just fine. What happened? What did I do?"

She dropped her head to look at the ground, and I didn't think she was going to answer me. Finally, she looked at me and shook her head. "I don't do this."

"Do what?"

"Flings," she answered. "I don't do relationships. I just don't think I'm cut out for that kind of thing. I told you I like my freedom. I don't want strings, and while I know you aren't trying to put a ring on my finger, you're only here for a short time. I don't want to get into this thing and then you leave and I'm left feeling weird."

"Weird?" I questioned.

"I like you, Ethan. I do, but I don't want to get into something that's never going to happen. My parents married for love. To hear them talk about it, they were young and naïve and fell head over heels. Then reality hit, and my mom left my dad. She destroyed him and our family. My dad never remarried. He never had another girlfriend. She crushed him. He died alone in that aspect. He didn't live long enough to really get over her. He died with a broken heart. My mom never really found love again either. I don't want to go through that. I don't know what a healthy relationship looks like. I don't know how to do it. I don't know what's good or bad. I don't know what's settling and what's compromising for love."

"I get it," I said. "I'm not looking for anything. I don't have the best examples to model after either. My parents are still married, but I wouldn't call it a loving relationship. It's a business arrangement. They stay married because divorce would cause a scandal. I'm not trying to put any pressure on you. I'm not trying to put pressure on me either. I wasn't looking for anything when I came here, but I'm not going to lie, I like spending time with you. You're different than any woman I've dated. I don't think we have to define anything, do we? Can't we just hang out and enjoy each other's company?"

"I think what just happens proves we can't," she said.

"We're two adults that are attracted to each other," I reasoned. "We didn't do anything wrong."

"No, but still."

"Okay, let me take you out on a real date," I said. "We've been spending all this time together because of a business arrangement. I can understand how that might make this feel a little weird. Why don't we just try a date and see how it goes? If things go well, we can revisit the dating thing. I'm not looking for anything, but that doesn't mean I didn't find something. Please, one dinner."

She looked like she was going to tell me to get lost. I waited, searching my brain for another angle. I didn't give up. I was used to negotiating with some tough people. I was good at getting people to do what I wanted. I made sure they understood how beneficial it was for them. Mutually beneficial.

"Okay," she finally said. "One date."

I grinned, unable to hide my excitement. "Tomorrow night?"

"Fine."

"I'll pick you up," I said.

"This is probably a really bad idea," she muttered.

"No idea is bad," I corrected. "Sometimes there are bad elements, but it's never just bad."

I got back into the car and headed for the house. She was someone I wanted to see again. Something about her grounded me. I felt so normal when I was with her. I knew I couldn't hide in Hawaii forever, but I needed just a little more. It wasn't just the sex. It was her. Everything about her.

Whatever we had wasn't real. I knew that. If I pursued something with her, she was going to figure out who I was. Once she did, she was going to drop me like a hot potato. I would have no defense. She'd made it clear she didn't like my family. I never admitted to being a member of the family she despised. The lie by omission was going to come back and bite me in the ass. I knew it, but I wasn't doing a damn thing to stop it. I shouldn't take her out on a date. I shouldn't want her at all. It was going to blow up in my face, and I had no one to blame but myself.

Chapter Twenty

Ava

"Where do you think he's going to take you?" Cindy asked.

I poured another cup of coffee. "I don't know. He just texted and said to dress nice."

"What are you going to wear?" she asked. "I don't think I've ever seen you dolled up."

"Because I don't get dolled up," I scoffed. "I think the last time I wore a dress was to my dad's funeral."

"It'll be fun," she said. "It's nice to dress up sometimes. Have fun with it. You're going to knock his socks off."

Or his pants. "I hope so," I said. "I just think I have to be very careful. He's my tenant."

"He's a man first," she said. "A hot man. So hot."

"Stop," I laughed.

"You need this," she said. "You need a good man in your life."

"He's not in my life," I corrected. "He's here for a short time. Then it's over."

"Maybe." She shrugged. "Maybe not."

"Definitely not," I insisted.

I finished my shift and headed home with thoughts of him on my mind. I knew it was a bad idea. Ethan was not the kind of guy I was going to forget anytime soon. The sex was bad enough. Going on a date with him and letting him turn on all that charm was dangerous. I already knew I was crazy about him. I had let myself get tangled up with a man I couldn't have. It was exactly what I had been trying to avoid. Figures it would happen with someone like him.

I called Andrea. I knew what she was going to tell me. I supposed I was looking for her approval. "Talk me off the ledge," I said when she answered.

"Uh-oh," she laughed. "What naughty thing are you about to do?"

"I slept with Ethan," I confessed immediately.

"Ha! I knew it! I knew you were hot for the dude. How was it?"

"That's not the point," I said with a sigh. "I can't do this with him. He's going to break my heart. I can already feel the cracks."

"Why do you think he's going to break your heart?" she asked.

"Because he's going back to New York soon," I said. "He's going back to that life, and I'm going to be here. I'm sure he'll say he's going to call and we'll keep in touch. Blah, blah, blah. I'm just the girl he fucked in Hawaii."

"I think that's a little presumptuous," she said.

"Maybe, but it doesn't change anything," I sighed. "He's some hot shot. He can't move here, and I'm definitely not moving there. It will never work. The long distance thing is a joke. Everyone knows that. I let myself fall into bed with him, and now I'm going on a date with him."

"It's usually the other way around," she laughed.

"Exactly. I'm a ho."

"You are so far from a ho you could practically live in a convent," she teased. "You finally did something normal."

"And now I'm going to pay the price. I don't know why I'm stressed. I don't want a boyfriend. I don't want a relationship at all. This thing we're doing is weird. I don't get it. We're not friends. We're not dating."

"Ah, but you want it to be more," she said. "You like him. That's why you're freaking out. You like him, and you're trying to figure out how you can make it work."

"No, because I know it won't work," I corrected her. "I'm going to fall for a guy I will never have. Then I'm going to be bitter and sulking. I don't want a broken heart. But on the flipside, I don't want a relationship. I don't want to answer to anyone. I'm so screwed up. I blame my parents. They doomed me to fail in the relationship department. Actually, I blame my mother because I know my father still loved her until the day he died. He was in it for the long haul. She screwed him over."

"And because she was rich you think Ethan is going to do to you what your mom did to your dad," she surmised.

"I suppose I am," I admitted. "It's not completely off base. I think he sees me as someone to occupy his time while he's hiding from his family. He might even like me a little, but that doesn't mean it could ever be more than that. He's not going to care that I have a broken heart."

"I think you're a pretty good judge of character," she said. "If you really thought this guy was a cad, you wouldn't even be thinking about him. But obviously, you know he's not, which is why you're struggling. You think he's a good guy, and you want him, but you're afraid of something that might not happen. You're not giving him or you a fair chance."

"You're saying I should go out with him and stop overthinking it," I said.

"And you know that's exactly what you should do," she laughed. "That's why you called me. You know what I'm going to say."

"I did."

"Stop trying to keep yourself from falling into the love trap," she said. "It's bound to happen one of these days. This might be that one in a billion shot at the real thing. I think you have to take the risk and find out for sure. Yes, it might blow up in your face. Yes, you might eat four gallons of ice cream after he breaks your heart, but that's just the way it is. You liked the sex, right?"

A little shudder snaked down my spine at the thought of it. "Yes."

"Then why not see what might happen?" she asked. "If he goes back to New York and you never see him again, I promise you'll heal. You're going to be able to look back on this little episode and laugh. You're going to be able to say you lived. You tried and you failed. The trying is half the fun. I'm still trying. Speaking of, I've got a date with a guy tonight that might be the one."

I rolled my eyes. "You say that about all of the men you go out with."

"Because I never know if it's going to be right," she replied. "I have to go out with the guy to find out if he's my soul mate. Unfortunately, the Creator didn't think to put some kind of mark on their foreheads so we could identify them. We have to actually meet them and go through the trouble of getting to know them before we figure it out."

"I think all that hiking turned you into one of those introspective people," I said.

"Maybe," she laughed. "Just try it. If you go out on this date with him and you realize he's better off as a friend or an acquaintance you'll never see again, so be it. You used to love risk. Get out there and live."

"Yeah, yeah," I muttered. "Now I have to figure out what to wear. I have a feeling he's going to take me somewhere expensive."

"Do you still have that black silk dress?" she asked. "I know you didn't get rid of it. That's what you should wear, assuming it hasn't been eaten by moths."

"I do have it," I said. A vision of it appeared in my mind. It was a gorgeous dress, and I loved the way I felt in it.

"There you go," she said. "Have fun."

I hung up and turned on the light in my closet. In the back, there was a garment bag with the few things I'd kept from my old life. My life in New York had included lots of designer dresses and expensive shoes. I was encouraged to go shopping. I spent like there was no end to the money train. When I moved to Hawaii, I sold off pieces here and there. When Dad got sick and money got tight, I sold more. But there were a few things I couldn't bring myself to sell.

I unzipped the bag and pulled out the black Prada. It was too fancy to wear anywhere here. My life was not about that anymore. I had simplified and figured out what was important. Prada and Gucci were no longer important to me. I sniffed the dress to make sure it didn't stink like mildew. I hung it on the back of the door and opened the shoebox with the Louboutin strappy sandals with the killer heel. I stepped back and admired the dress with the draping neckline. I supposed if I was being honest, I could admit I missed some parts of my old life. I used to love getting dressed up and going to the clubs. I had been so young and carefree. It was hard to believe that life was only a mere five years ago. It felt like a lifetime.

I showered and lathered my skin with lotion. I took my time with my makeup, pulling out pallets that had not seen the light of day in forever. I had fun putting on the makeup and doing my hair in an updo. Then I slid the dress over my body. The silk brushed over my skin and thankfully still fit perfectly. I sat down and put on the shoes before inspecting the look in the mirror. I knew what I needed to complete the look. I opened my top dresser drawer and pulled out the black box I had been given on my eighteenth birthday.

My grandmother had been nice to me. I didn't necessarily agree with everything she stood for, but we got along. I opened the box with the diamond earrings. They were worth a fortune. My dad was the one that had convinced me to keep them. He insisted I pass them down to my own daughter one day. I carefully put them on and felt complete. I was certain I looked like the kind of woman Ethan would date back in New York. He was not going to believe his eyes when he saw me.

He arrived right on time. "Holy shit," he said when I opened the door.

"I hope that's holy shit in a good way."

He bobbed his head up and down. "It definitely is. You're stunning."

"Thank you," I replied. "I clean up pretty well."

"I would say more than just a little."

He looked devastating in his expensive suit that I knew had been tailored just for him. It fit perfectly. The shoes looked expensive as well.

I was guessing handcrafted in Italy. My grandfather was all about his Italian shoes. He was convinced they made the best.

"You look nice," I said. "Very Bond-like."

He smirked and tugged at the hem of the jacket. "This old thing?"

"Very funny. Did you bring that with you?"

"I did." He nodded. "I wasn't sure if I would have a need for a suit, but just in case. I'm glad I did. I would never be able to take you out in that dress in anything less."

"Thank you."

"You really are beautiful," he said. He leaned in and kissed me on the cheek. It was the perfect gentlemanly thing to do. There was no passion. It was just a proper kiss. "Are you ready?"

"Yes, but let me make sure Roxy has water."

I was suddenly nervous. It was an actual date. I knew it, but to be dressed up and have him in front of me made it all real. I had to remember all my manners. This was the real thing. He opened the car door for me like a gentleman. Sitting in the Porsche in my Prada dress took me back to New York. I had convinced myself I would never do this kind of thing again, but here I was.

He looked over at me after starting the engine. "Something wrong?" I asked.

He smiled and shook his head. "Just the opposite."

He pulled away but kept stealing looks. I was beginning to wonder if I had a booger hanging out or something. The man was looking at me like I was a freak. Was he really expecting me to wear my cutoff jean shorts? Maybe he thought I was perpetually in jeans with no makeup. When we got to the restaurant, my stomach erupted into butterflies. It was extremely expensive. There were rumors a certain former president frequented the place. The person I was now didn't belong in a place so fancy. My old self did. She was who I was going to have to rely on to get me through dinner without embarrassing myself and my date.

Chapter Twenty-One

Ethan

I couldn't stop staring at her. I knew I was being rude, but damn. She was gorgeous. I knew she was pretty. She was pretty and beautiful without the designer dress and makeup, but seeing her now was a gut punch in the best way. She had taken my breath away when she opened the door.

"All right, what is it?" she asked.

"What?"

"You're staring at me again," she said. "I went to the powder room, and I don't see what you're looking at."

"You," I answered. "I'm looking at you. I think you're pretty hot every other day of the week, but you are stunning."

She touched her hair. "I don't usually do this."

I had sensed her discomfort the moment we sat down. She was uncomfortable in the restaurant. When it was time to order drinks, I saw her eyeing the beer menu, but she stopped herself. She ordered a glass of wine instead.

"Drink wine or get dressed up?" I teased.

"Both," she laughed nervously. "I feel like there is a spotlight directed at me. I don't want to do something stupid."

"There isn't a spotlight," I assured her. "And you don't need to fear doing anything stupid. It's a meal. We've shared countless meals together. You've never been nervous."

"That was different."

"How so?" I asked.

"Because no one cared what I was wearing there," she said. "No one was going to be judging me. I think you know what these people are like."

"What people?"

She gestured with her hand. "Wealthy people," she whispered. "They look at people like me and wonder what I'm doing in their space. It's my own insecurities. I'm sure no one cares who I am. Old habits and all that."

Her history was a mystery. She mentioned growing up wealthy, or at least part of her childhood had been wealthy. "We can go somewhere else," I suggested.

"No." She shook her head. "We're here. I'll be fine. Like I said, it's my own insecurities getting the best of me."

"For what it's worth, anyone looking at you isn't going to be judging you; they're going to be admiring you. It's more than just the dress and the perfect hair. You have a confidence about you that is admirable. You glow. I was drawn to it the first time I met you."

"You were kicking me out of the house the first time we met," she said with a small laugh.

"Okay, true, but that had nothing to do with you and everything to do with me," I said. "I was trying to hide, but I did see your beauty. The beauty inside and out."

"That's very sweet." She smiled.

"It's true," I said. "If you want to go, we can. I really don't mind."

"No way," she said. "I've heard this place is really good. If we're here, we might as well enjoy it."

"For the price, it better be," I joked.

I had a feeling the cost of the food was based on the view. It was gorgeous. The full moon was low in the sky, casting a beautiful reflection on the water that was nice and smooth. I could understand why people paid millions of dollars for tiny little homes on the beach. The view was worth it.

"Do you like seafood?" I asked her. "Or is that obvious?"

"I do like seafood." She nodded. "I'm not a picky eater."

"I saw the pictures of your dad fishing," I said. "Did you do a lot of fishing with him?"

"I wouldn't say a lot." She smiled. "I went out with him sometimes. I was usually moral support. I did not inherit the fishing gene. I could have my line in the water all day and never catch anything. My dad did. He was a great fisherman. He showed me how to clean and fillet his catches. We would build fires right on the beach and eat pan fried fish."

"That sounds amazing," I said.

"It was."

"Your dad lived a full life," I continued.

"He did." She nodded thoughtfully as she sipped her wine. "He was kind of a burly dude, but he had the softest, most gentle soul. He found beauty in everything. He got to see most of the world during his time in the Navy, but here is where he said he belonged. I don't think he would have lived as long had he not been here. He would have given up. His heart was here. His bed was facing the window. He would spend hours staring outside. When I could, we got him into his wheelchair. I used to watch him from the window, worried about him. He would sit on the deck in the sun and a smile on his face. He was a simple man. I think he would have been perfectly happy living on a deserted island in a hut."

"Before this last week, I would have said I didn't understand that. After spending time here, I get it. I've never been a nature boy. I don't think I'll ever be your dad's level of nature boy, but being here and visiting the waterfalls and just being on the beach is restorative. I wasn't sick, but I feel like I've been healing."

I had never said anything so cheesy in all my life, but it was all true. That's what made her so special. I could say that to her and not feel like a complete moron. She got it. I knew she would understand. She had gone through her own healing.

"I know exactly what you mean." She smiled. "I think the people who can let go of the material things in life will find true happiness here. People that are still attached to the material world might see the beauty, but they'll never truly understand the healing properties of nature. My friend Andrea just went on a backpacking trip across Europe. She's different now. I haven't seen her, but the transformation in her was pretty obvious. At the start of the trip, she was posting on social media with a full face of makeup. It was all about selling an idea. As the trip progressed, she posted less, and she was more natural. I'm happy for her. We each went on our own journeys. Everyone has to find what works for them."

"This is working for me," I said. "Little by little, things are changing for me."

"I've noticed," she said.

"You have?"

She rubbed her jaw. "This is a change."

I grinned and rubbed at the scruff on my face. "I always wanted to wear facial hair. I couldn't do it in the military. Then when I got out, it was straight into the corporate world. My family has some pretty strict dress standards. If they saw me now, they would not be pleased."

"I like it," she said. "Oddly enough, it softens your appearance."

I frowned. "I'm not sure that was the look I was going for."

"Not soft like weak—soft as in approachable. You look like a guy that doesn't mind getting sand on his feet or eating macadamia nut pancakes."

"Then my look suits me," I laughed.

"Will you keep it when you go back?" she asked.

"I'm not sure," I admitted.

"Do you work in the city?" she asked.

I had to be careful. It wouldn't be hard for her to connect the dots between who I was and who my family was. The moment she did, I had a feeling she would be out of the restaurant before I could get out of my chair. It was dangerous ground I was treading on. "I do, but I can work from anywhere," I quickly added.

"What do you do?"

I shrugged and took a drink to stall for time. "I'm in the corporate world. We basically move money around to make people richer."

"Ah, you are in the Wall Street business." She smiled. "I knew it when I saw you. I felt bad for judging you, but I think I nailed it."

"Maybe a little," I laughed.

We ordered the Kona lobster with all the sides. She drank two glasses of wine while I stuck to club soda. I was glad to see her relaxing a little. I felt a little guilty for bringing her to a restaurant that made her uncomfortable.

"It's so good," she whispered. "I guess you have to take the ambiance if you want to eat the gourmet food."

"Is it worth it?" I asked.

She nodded. "Totally. Only because you're here. I don't think I would be able to enjoy this with anyone else."

"Thank you." I nodded. "I appreciate that. Do you want to get dessert?"

"I think I'm okay," she said.

"Why don't we get something to go," I suggested.

"That sounds like a good idea."

We ordered the signature lava cake to go. It was a tricky moment. I wasn't sure if I should take her back to her place or suggest we go to the rental house. I gauged her mood and figured I may as well take a chance. "How about a nightcap?" I asked. "I know a place with a great view."

"Oh you do?" she teased.

"Yes." I nodded. "It's got a very comfortable deck with total privacy."

She laughed again. "I think that sounds like a very good idea."

I drove us back to the house. The bar was moderately stocked. I had picked up a few bottles over the week. Ava took off her shoes and meandered out to the deck. I watched her put her hands on the railing and stare into the backyard. I wondered why she didn't move into the house. She loved it. The place was very her. It was surrounded by nature, which I knew she loved.

I carried the drinks to the deck and handed her one. "It's so nice out here," she said softly. "Do you come out here at night?"

"I do."

"Good." She nodded. "This place deserves to be appreciated."

"Did you ever stay the night here?" I asked.

"Once." She smiled. "Time had gotten away from me. Instead of driving home, I crashed on the floor in the living room. I did get to see the sunrise from the deck. It was stunning. I knew whoever stayed here would get to see the real beauty of the island."

"It's a beautiful home," I told her. "You've done a great job with your real estate choices."

She laughed and looked at me in the moonlight. "Thank you."

"Are you going to buy more?"

"I don't know," she answered. "I might. I've been lucky so far, but I've heard plenty of horror stories. I have to buy cheap and then do the work myself. Unfortunately, with the market right now, there isn't anything cheap. I'm just biding my time."

"Very smart."

We both stared into the darkness. I was trying to tamp down the desire. I didn't want to make a move and have her shut down again. I was willing to wait for her to come to me. If she didn't want me, I would accept it. I would rather keep her as a friend than lose her from my life altogether.

We finished our drinks. "Can I get you another?" I asked.

She put her glass on the small patio table. I watched her walk back toward me slowly and seductively. I didn't move. I didn't breathe. I felt the change in her. She reached up and put her hand on the back of my neck. Her body slid against mine. I was doing a chant in my head, telling myself not to touch. It was like a wild animal coming in close. One wrong move and she would run away.

"Ethan," she breathed.

"Yes?"

She rose up and kissed me. I let her dictate the heat. When her tongue swiped across my lips, I opened my mouth and got into the game. I wasn't the type to sit back and let someone run the show. She'd initiated the kiss. That was enough for me.

My hands slid down her sides and over her hips. I reached for her ass and pulled her against my erection. Her hands slid down my back. I enjoyed the sensuality of the moment. The moonlight made it all the better. The kissing was hot and wet and just a little messy. I slid my tongue over her jaw and sucked on her neck. Her back arched, leaning back with my arms wrapped around her waist and holding her close. My tongue moved around to her throat, licking and nibbling before following the neckline of the dress down to her cleavage. I nibbled at her flesh through the lace bra. Her sweet moans were music to my ears.

Just when I was getting to the point of no return, I pulled back. "Ava, do you want to stop?" I asked breathlessly.

"No," she answered.

"You're sure?" I asked with my body demanding I shut my mouth and take her to bed.

She reached between us and grabbed my cock. "I'd really like to go inside now."

She didn't have to tell me twice.

Chapter Twenty-Two

Ava

I followed him upstairs to the master bedroom. It smelled like him. I could feel his presence all around. He stopped me and pulled at my dress. I turned to give him my back. He slid the zipper down and let the dress fall away. I stepped out of it, and when I turned to face him, he was pulling off his shirt in a hurry. I watched the strip tease with my lower lip between my teeth.

"Damn," I said when he was down to his briefs.

He stopped stripping and looked at me. "See something you like?"

"I definitely do," I said. "Please tell me you've got condoms here."

"Two seconds."

He walked to his suitcase and pulled one out. I snatched it from his hand. "Let's just keep that there for a second."

He stepped toward me and grabbed me against him. "Do you know how sexy you are?" he asked.

"No, but I know you make me feel very sexy," I said.

"You're incredible." He ran a hand over my breast. "Your body is amazing. I'm just going to say it; you've got some really, really nice tits."

I laughed at the statement. I pulled at his face and demanded he kiss me. He slid his hand up and unhooked my bra. We stripped naked and fell into bed. I pushed him down and climbed over him. I wanted to get a good look at the man. I straddled him, running my hands over his chest. The muscles rippled under my hands.

"You know when we were on the beach the other day, I could think of nothing but touching you. You've gotten quite the tan since you've been here." I leaned down and kissed one of his flat nipples. Then the other.

"You should have," he said. "Trust me, I never would have rejected your touch. Your anything."

I kissed down his stomach. "I see that."

I slid my body down his legs and kissed his belly. The muscles flexed under my lips. I kept going down. I wrapped my hand around his cock and gently pulled. I kissed the tip. He gasped and jerked. I held on to his cock and slid my mouth down his full length. He let out a loud groan. I sucked harder, listening to his grunts and groans. His hands moved to my hair, pulling it from the clips and weaving his fingers between the strands. He massaged my scalp and pulled my head down. I could feel his excitement rising.

Suddenly, he was lifting me over him. He rolled over and pinned me to the mattress beneath him. "You turn me inside out," he growled.

I reached out and grabbed the condom. He quickly put it on and pushed inside me with one hard thrust. Sucking on him and driving him crazy had turned me on more than I anticipated. I frantically grabbed at him, kissing and pulling him against me. I suddenly couldn't get enough of him. I wanted the man more than breath. I loved what he did to my body.

He moved fast and hard. The bed rocked and squeaked. I clawed at him. We hit the peak together. He pulled me against him while our bodies spasmed and jerked. He fell beside me and grabbed me against him. He held me tightly like he was afraid I might sneak away. I supposed after the last time we were together, his fears were reasonable.

"You know what?" he asked.

"I'm afraid to ask."

"We still have that chocolate cake downstairs," he said. "I don't know about you, but I really want some of that cake."

"Craving something sweet?" I teased.

"I already had something sweet," he replied.

I laughed and kissed his chin. I could barely move. He had me wrapped up tightly. "Should we go get some?"

"I was thinking cake and brandy," he said. "I bought a bottle a few days ago and have been enjoying it at night while I appreciate the view from the deck."

"Oh, that does sound very good."

We climbed out of bed. He tossed his shirt at me to put on. He wore just his underwear. I cut the cake while he poured us glasses of brandy, and we ate at the kitchen table. "Isn't it nice to hear nothing?" I commented.

"Honestly, the first few nights, it was hard to sleep," he said. "I kept waiting for a siren. It was too quiet. But the sounds of the bugs and critters felt so loud."

"A lot of people like the idea of renting near the beach to listen to the sound of the ocean," I said. "I don't think people realize how loud the ocean can be."

"I believe it," he said. "I debated between your house and a house on the beach. The house on the beach was gorgeous, and I thought it might be fun to walk out the back door down the beach. Then I realized I could stick my hand out the window and touch the neighbor's house. I decided privacy and solitude was more popular than hearing the ocean."

"I made another assumption about you when you first got here," I said.

"I'm afraid to ask."

I laughed and pointed my fork at him. "I suspected you were hiding from someone or something. I had some fantasies about you hiding from the mob or the police."

"Sorry," he said with a shake of his head. "Just my family. Although I think they could give the mob a run for their money."

"Do they know you're out here?" I asked.

He shook his head and revealed a slow smile. "Nope. I'm not trying to sound like a cocky asshole, but I have a private jet. I didn't want my family or anyone else to be able to track it. I charted a plane under a different name."

I raised an eyebrow. "You really are hiding."

"I am."

"Do you want to tell me why?" I asked, suspecting he didn't want to.

"I just needed to get away from the craziness of my life," he said. "I couldn't think. They are always there. It wouldn't matter to them if I told them I needed a couple days off. They would impose on my time. I had to get away. This was the only way I could think to shut off the noise."

I suspected there was a lot more going on. Something had sent him running. I wasn't going to pry. If and when he was ready to tell me, I would listen. I told myself I wouldn't judge, but I had a feeling that was a lot easier said than done.

"I don't want to assume, but would you like to stay here tonight?" he asked. "If you don't want to, I'll take you home. No pressure."

"I would love to stay," I answered. "Although, if I'm sleeping here, is it fair for me to charge you for tonight's stay?"

He laughed and swatted my ass as we headed upstairs. "You're not my landlord right now. You're—"

"I'm—?" I asked.

"You're my guest," he replied.

We both stripped naked once again and climbed into bed together. He snuggled me close. I wanted to believe this was all real. It felt real. He was a great guy, the kind of man I knew I could very easily fall in love with. We had a deep connection. We had only known each other a very short time, but it felt like so much longer. When we were together, it was easy to imagine a future with him. He was easy to talk to, and I truly felt like he understood me. We did have a few things in common, like the pushy family back in New York. I did notice neither of us liked to talk much about our families.

He seemed to be falling in love with my home. He certainly had the money to buy his own place in Oahu. He said he could work from anywhere. What if there was a chance he would decide to pick up and move here? The thought scared me. I both wanted it and was terrified by it. I was still leery of a relationship. But if it was with someone like Ethan who seemed to appreciate the idea of being free, it might not be so scary.

I was confused. He confused me. He made me want things I didn't think I wanted. He made me feel things. If I let myself think of a future with him, I saw happiness. I saw us exploring every inch of every island in Hawaii. We would make love in the waterfalls and on the prettiest mountaintops. We could make such beautiful memories together.

But was that what he wanted? I was getting way ahead of myself. I forced myself to close my eyes and try to sleep. I needed the rest.

Chapter Twenty-Three

Ethan

I stretched and reached for Ava only to find an empty bed. My eyes popped open and quickly closed again. The sun was streaming through the window. I opened my eyes once again. After verifying the bed was empty, I got up and pulled on my underwear. I hoped she was downstairs. I felt the emptiness in the house immediately.

She'd left without saying a word, which stung a little. I couldn't quite figure her out. She was hot and cold, and I didn't know where I fell into the mix. I realized we had yet to really talk about this thing between us. She probably thought I was using her for sex. I wasn't. I wasn't sure what we were, but we were never going to figure it out if we didn't talk about it.

But that was where things got tricky. I didn't know how to talk about it because I didn't know where my life was going. I might find myself embroiled in a scandal that she would not want anything to do with. That would lead to her finding out who my family was. I couldn't really talk to her about dating. I couldn't give her anything. I didn't know what I had to offer besides a lot of drama.

I decided to go for a run. It would help clear my head and point me in the right direction. I hit the beach and felt the same feeling of happiness I got every time the beach came into view. While I ran, I thought about her. I didn't know what I could offer her, but I could be straight with her. She deserved that much. I would be honest and tell her I did have feelings for her, but I was not in a place to commit to anything. She was a good person, and I didn't want her to think I was using her.

I hoped we could keep some kind of friendship after I left. I might find myself needing a hiding spot again very soon.

I made it back to the house and thought about calling her, then I realized she was probably at work. "Duh," I said with relief. I didn't even ask her if she had to work this morning. She was at the coffee shop. I wasn't going to panic and freak out over her leaving me without a goodbye. She might have said goodbye and I was dead asleep.

Feeling better about everything, I went for my usual shower. While drinking my coffee, I actually felt ready to finally do a little work. There was enough distance between us that I was cool with checking in. I took my coffee to the table and looked around. I'd had my laptop yesterday. I thought I had it on the table. I jogged upstairs and looked in the bedroom. It wasn't there.

"What the hell?"

I searched the usual spots and even looked out on the patio table just in case I might have left it out there. I was about to pull my hair out when I got a phone call. I hoped it was Ava. I rushed into the kitchen to grab it only to see it was Lucas. I hadn't talked to my best friend since I'd flown the coop. I suspected my parents were hounding the shit out of him. He would give me the space. He had to be calling because something was up. He was on the board of the company as well. I had given him a heads-up I was going to be taking some time off. I trusted him to keep his mouth shut.

"Hello," I answered.

"Enjoying your vacation?" he asked.

"Yes, actually, I am," I said.

"Sorry to burst your bubble, but you should turn on the TV."

"Why?" I asked.

"CNN," he said. "Trust me, you have to see this to believe it."

Dread flooded me. I walked to the living room and turned on the TV. I quickly found CNN. It was my brother's face on the screen. "Shit," I muttered. "I'll call you back."

I turned up the volume. The reporter who had been hounding me the last couple of weeks was on air. Marta Mikkels was worse than a dog with a bone. She was ruthless. Her reputation was not great. She was unscrupulous. She fancied herself some major news journalist when she was really just a pain in the ass. A real journalist would stay within the lines. She was obnoxious. No one trusted her. When she showed up anywhere, everyone shut down.

"Collin Mitchell has recently launched his campaign to become a member of Congress," Marta said in her obnoxious reporter voice. "Collin is the youngest son of the influential Mitchell family. He was once thought to be a rising star in the world of politics, but that star might have just fizzled out. I have been researching this story for weeks. I have learned that Collin, who has quite the reputation..."

"Fuck you," I growled.

"Collin has lived up to the idea of being the spare to the heir of the Mitchell throne," she went on. "We've all covered the stories on Collin. The guy likes to party. Unfortunately, it looks like his latest party binge cost someone their life. We can't name the victim here yet, but we do know the young man was a close friend of Collin Mitchell's. We know Collin was caught with some party drugs along with the young socialite he was out with. From what I've learned, Collin and the victim were together for most of the night. There was drinking and drug use. The friend was found just after two in the morning. Attempts to revive him were unsuccessful. What we don't know was whether or not Collin Mitchell was present at the time of the man's death. There are a lot of rumors and speculation about who made the call to the police. My source tells me Collin was there and fled the scene before police arrived to avoid being questioned."

I listened to Marta go on about details that no one knew. Details we were keeping within the family. Only myself, my parents, and Collin knew. And the lawyer. Someone was talking.

I called Lucas back after the segment was over. Lucas was privy to the details as well. He was practically a member of the family. He had been apprised of the situation in case the story broke. I thought it was being clamped down.

"I don't know," Lucas answered. "We knew shit was heating up, but we don't know what the hell is happening."

"Who's talking to the reporter?" I asked.

"I don't know," he said. "As far as I know, no one knew she was going to air the story today. We thought it was still in the fact-finding stage."

"When have facts ever been an issue for that woman?" I growled. "Have you talked with my family?"

"Are you kidding me?" he laughed. "My ears are burning. I've got calls on hold. Shit is blowing up, man. You need to be here. I'm not going to ask where you are, but I don't think we can keep this under control much longer."

"Under control," I said. "It isn't under control. It's on the fucking news!"

"You knew it was coming," he said.

"Did she talk to someone at the office? Who is talking? She knows the names of those involved. She knew where he was that night. How did that happen?"

"I don't know," he said. "Your parents are freaking out."

"Does his family know?" I asked.

"Hell no," Lucas said. "No one knows anything. The girl, Jenny, she knows. I don't think she's talking. It would incriminate her as well."

I shook my head. There was nothing for me to do there. I couldn't stop the story. It was happening. It was out there. Collin had made his shitty choices. He kept making them. He wasn't learning a lesson. He was never going to learn if he kept getting away with this shit.

"I don't know," I said. "I don't know what to do. I don't think there is anything I can do."

"The story is out there now," he sighed. "The best we can do is find the leak and seal it."

"No one else knows," I said aloud. I was trying to think of who else. Who had something to gain from any of this? "What about the girl?" I asked. "Is someone looking into her?"

"Yes," Lucas said. "I got an email asking about enemies that might have something to gain for taking down Collin and the company."

"Email?"

"Yes, the team of lawyers working on this thing," he said. "They wanted to know if the girl might be connected to someone. Like an inside takedown."

"Oh shit," I murmured. Pieces were falling into place. Ava. Ava had been at the house, and now my laptop was missing.

"What's wrong?" Lucas asked. "What do you know?"

"It's not what I know, it's my laptop," I said. "It went missing last night. Maybe this morning. I've been seeing a girl. I don't know the specifics, but she mentioned she had a serious beef with the Mitchell family from New York. I assumed she didn't know who I was. She never let on she did. In fact, she said she was glad I wasn't a part of the family. She stayed the night. I woke up this morning, and she was gone. And so is my laptop."

"Fuck!" I heard a thud and knew he'd either thrown something or hit something. "Are you serious?"

"I've been looking for my laptop," I said. "I swear I left it on the kitchen table. It isn't there. I've searched. It's gone. My email is logged in. The information that's out there would have been in my emails. Someone would be able to get those emails."

"Where the hell are you?" he asked.

"Oahu," I confessed. "Please don't tell anyone. I'm renting a house here. The landlord is the woman I've been spending time with."

He let out a long sigh. "Who is she?" he asked.

"Her name is Ava Hunt," I said. "She didn't tell me specifics, but she said something about my family making her family lose all their money. But I don't get it. She told me she didn't have anything to do with her family in New York."

"And you believed her?" he scoffed.

"I don't know." I rubbed my head. "I don't know what to think. Maybe she knew who I was when I booked the reservation. Maybe someone found out where I was and got to her. I don't know what to think. I'm feeling a little blindsided. I can't believe she would do this. This can't be right."

"What else is on the laptop?" he asked.

"She can't get into the company stuff," I said. "That requires passwords. My email. My Amazon. Maybe my Netflix. There's nothing too important on there. At least not anything that would hurt the company."

"Your brother has done plenty to hurt the company," he muttered. "You need to get the laptop back."

"Does it even matter at this point?" I asked. "Seriously, the damage is done. Anyone with half a brain would have already made copies. I doubt I can just ask for it and get it back. She's never going to hand it over."

"We may have to pursue legal options," he said. "Right now, we're up a creek. The information is out there. I need to talk with the rest of the board. I'm going to look into this woman."

"I'm going to track her down myself," I said.

"You should probably leave it alone," he warned. "There's no good that can come from it at this point. She fucked you, literally and figuratively. Don't give her another reason to come after you. Just leave her alone. You might want to think about getting your ass on a plane and getting back here."

"I'm not coming back," I said. "No way. I don't want to be forced to answer questions outside the company headquarters. That just gives them a way to connect Collin to the company. Right now, it's a tenuous connection."

"You're going to keep renting from the woman that threw you to the wolves?" he asked.

"I don't know," I said. "I'm not sure what I'm going to do, but I'm not going back there. This shitstorm happens whether I'm there or not. I can only try and mitigate the damage to the company. I can do that from here."

"Watch your back," he said. "The vultures are circling. If she's spying on you, they know where you are. Your little island paradise is going to be public knowledge very soon."

"Thanks," I muttered. "I'll check in later. For now, I need to handle my business."

I ended the call, barely resisting the temptation to throw the damn phone across the room. I had been a damn fool. I let her good looks and sweet girl image fool me. She'd played me. The betrayal was the worst feeling I had ever experienced. It tasted bitter and nasty. Worst of all, it hurt. My stomach physically hurt. People lied to me all the time. That wasn't a big deal. It was the fact she let me think there was some kind of bond between us. I truly believed we had something special. I thought she might care about me.

To find out it was all a means to an end really hurt. I wasn't sure I would ever recover.

Chapter Twenty-Four

Ava

"You seriously look like a woman that is floating," Cindy said. "You are so happy."

I flashed her a grin. "I am happy."

"Does this mean you're giving the relationship a chance?" she asked. "And don't pretend you don't know what I'm talking about. You are so smitten with this guy. I'm happy for you. I like seeing you smile."

"Thank you," I said. "I'm not saying it's anything serious, but I think I've decided to just lean into it. I'll take what I can get. I've been second-guessing myself and trying to put everything into a box. Life isn't supposed to be neat and tidy. I might end up regretting it, but I guess that's the price I'll pay."

She put up her hand to give me a high-five. "Congratulations. Good for you."

There had been a steady stream of customers all morning. It was the weekend and people from the other islands were coming in to visit. I wasn't sure what I was going to be doing when I got off work, but I was pretty certain it was going to be with him. He had looked so sweet and relaxed when I left. His face looked a lot younger when he wasn't frowning. It had been so hard to get out of bed. I would have loved to wake up with him and spend a leisurely morning drinking coffee and doing nothing.

I made it through the shift and quickly rushed to the breakroom to get my things. I was already thinking about what we could do for the day. When I pulled up to my house, I was elated to see him waiting for me. I hopped out of the car, anxious to throw my arms around him. I stopped short when I saw the scowl on his face. He looked pissed.

"I didn't call," I said. "I'm sorry. I got busy at work and didn't have time to text."

"We need to talk," he said.

"Okay," I said. "Are you okay?"

"We need to talk."

"Okay, come in," I said. "I need to let Roxy out. Poor girl got shafted last night."

He said nothing. I felt he was overreacting just a little to me being gone when he woke up. He had to have known I worked this morning. I worked most mornings.

"Did you sleep okay?" I asked and opened the door. "You were dead to the world when I left this morning. I was just a little jealous."

He closed the door behind me. "I slept fine," he said in a gruff voice.

"Roxy," I greeted the dog. "Let's go outside."

I opened the back door for her and then rejoined Ethan. He was still scowling. "Do you want some water?" I asked. "I'm so thirsty."

"I don't want water."

I grabbed a glass and filled it from the pitcher. He looked furious and stressed out at the same time. He was frowning.

"What's up?" I asked.

That's when he finally looked at me. He turned his scowl on me. "What the fuck, Ava?"

I flinched and leaned back. "What?"

"How could you?"

"How could I what?" I asked. I was trying to keep my cool, but he was coming on pretty strong. I didn't appreciate his tone or his aggressiveness.

"I thought you were different," he said. "I never thought you would betray anyone, let alone me. I thought you were real. You fooled me. I'll give you that. Congrats."

"How did I fool you?" I asked with my arms folded across my chest.

"You made me let my guard down," he said. "You worked me. You got me to trust you. I've dealt with a lot of manipulative people, but this is next level. You could give a masterclass in it."

At first, I thought he was joking. But his face said anything but. He was pissed. He was furious.

"Okay, you need to take a beat and tell me what you are talking about," I said. "You've got a lot of anger going on."

"You think?" he scoffed. "Why would I possibly be angry? What could be the reason?"

"I don't know," I snapped. "That's why I'm asking you."

"Where's my laptop?" he growled.

"I don't know." I shrugged. "Why would I know that?"

"Who got to you?" he asked.

"Who got to me?" I asked with confusion. I studied him close. "Have you been on the beach? Did you fall asleep in the sun?"

"What the hell are you talking about?"

"You are not making any sense," I said. "Let me get you some water. I think you're dehydrated."

"I'm not fucking dehydrated," he said. "I want to know why. Why would you do this? I thought we connected. I thought you were different."

"Okay," I said calmly. He was furious. Shouting at him was not going to solve anything. I was going to be the calm one. Then maybe we could have an actual, coherent conversation. "I need to know what you are asking me. You're firing off a lot of questions, and none of them are making any sense to me."

"Where is my laptop?" he asked in a gruff tone.

I shook my head. "I don't know."

"You used me," he said. "You know who I am and thought you had an easy way to make a little money on the side. Was it the reporter? Someone else? I hope you're getting paid very well for fucking me over."

"I'm not fucking you over, and I'm certainly not getting paid to do it," I shot back.

"Do you still have the laptop, or did you turn it over to whoever convinced you to fuck me over?" he asked.

"Who in the hell would pay me to fuck you over?" I asked with confusion.

"Why the games?" he asked. "Why did you have to get in my head? You had the key. You could have taken the laptop when I was gone. You didn't have to fuck me. You didn't have to pretend you were my friend. What you did was cruel. I thought you were different. I thought you were the kind of person I could lean on. I should have known I couldn't trust you or anyone else. Everyone is out for themselves. I couldn't figure out why we clicked. I never click with anyone. Then you showed up, and it was like I had met my soul mate. But none of it was real, was it? You did your homework and figured out what it would take to buddy up to me. If you wanted to make a fool of me, good job. Thanks for reminding me there are no real people out there. Everyone wants something from Ethan Mitchell."

"Wow," I said. "Are you done?"

"No. I want my fucking laptop."

I threw my hands up. "I don't know why you're here bugging me about it," I said. Then it dawned on me. "Wait, you actually think I have your laptop?"

He gave me a hard look. "I think you probably handed it off."

"I never took you for crazy," I said. "I'm glad I'm learning this now."

"I'm not crazy."

"I think you might be," I said. "You've got some issues."

"Just give me the laptop," he sighed. "Or tell me who you gave it to. I don't know why you had to meddle. I have enough drama in my life. Was it really necessary to sleep with me?"

"I think you should go," I told him. "You're not someone I ever want to see again. You don't get to come into my house and accuse me of stealing anything from you. I've never stolen anything in my life. I don't know who you think I gave your laptop to. I didn't. Take your crazy ass out of my house now."

He turned to walk to the door and then stopped. The look he gave me gutted me. It was full of pain. "You could have just been straight. You could have just left me alone. You didn't have to do this."

"Ethan, I have no earthly idea what you are talking about, but I know you need to leave," I said calmly. "I don't care to see you ever again."

"My laptop," he said again.

"You fucking asshole! You were looking for a cord yesterday! I told you where I kept spares. There's a fucking charging station in the drawer in the kitchen. Remember? You've been using it to charge your phone. Did you even look there before you came rushing over here to accuse me of stealing something I don't want or need? Do you honestly think I'm that hard up I can't buy my own fucking laptop?" I stomped to the living room and snatched my own laptop. "Here, asshole. Would you like to take mine? Would that make you feel better?"

"I don't want yours. I want mine."

I was done. I had no more patience to deal with him. I pointed to the door. "Get out. Now. Don't you dare call me or show up here again. Your contract ends in two weeks. Please don't darken my door again."

He walked out of the apartment and slammed the door behind him. I didn't move. I couldn't. I was in complete shock by his behavior. It was insulting. The man was completely different than the man I had spent two weeks with. Last night we had really come together. I felt like we had shared something special. It killed me to have him throw it away without even thinking twice. He used me. I had let myself be used by a rich asshole from New York.

I had been so worried about getting close to him because I didn't want him to crush my heart. "Too late," I muttered.

I locked the front door. I didn't expect him to come back, but if he did, I didn't want to see him. I wanted him to stay far away from me. If I could have done it, I would have kicked him out of my house. I didn't want him in my house or on my island. His shady ass belonged in New York.

Chapter Twenty-Five

Ethan

I made it to the car before I stopped and actually heard the words she'd said. I did remember looking for a power cord. This morning in my frantic haste, I had not looked in the drawer. It was one of those drawers that wasn't a drawer. It had several USB connectors. It was a neat and tidy place to charge phones, tablets and laptops. I looked at her front door and realized I might have made a mistake.

I walked back to her door and knocked. "Go away!" she called out.

"Ava, let me talk to you," I said.

"You already did that," she shouted through the door.

"This is serious, Ava! Open the door!"

I pounded on it a few times and waited. She pulled open the door and glared at me. "I'm going to call the cops," she said.

"I didn't look in the drawer," I confessed.

"So?" she snapped.

"I just need to know, did you leak the information to the press?" I asked calmly.

She glared at me. "I don't know what you are talking about, but I swear, I will slam the door in your face if you don't leave. And I mean actually slam it with the hopes it will hit you in the nose."

"My laptop had information on it," I said. "It's missing. Suddenly, there is information out there that was on my laptop."

"Sucks to be you," she snapped. "You should really look before you leap. I didn't take your stupid laptop."

"Okay, but did you talk to the press?" I asked.

She started to shut the door. I put my foot out to block it. I stared into her eyes and searched for the answer. There was a flash of tears before I saw the same defiance I had seen earlier.

"I don't know what you are talking about," she said again. "You're a total jackass."

"Did they offer you money?" I asked.

She closed her eyes and took a deep breath. "You are crazy. I don't know what's wrong with you. I have no idea what makes you think you are that special. Why in the hell would I take money from anyone? Do you actually think I would sell your secrets? What secret would I sell, Ethan? Am I supposed to give them details about what you do in bed? Do you think I should tell them all the dirty details? Should I talk you up, say you have a big dick?"

"No," I said with disgust.

"You're reducing me to someone who talks to the media for money," she said. "Clearly you think that's what I'm about. You think I'm someone who likes to fuck around and talk. You disgust me. I knew I should have never got into bed with you. You're a pig."

I'd hurt her feelings. That was obvious. I was beginning to think I'd made a mistake. The laptop was likely in the drawer. Now that I had time to calm down, I realized it was pretty unlikely she would talk to the press. She was a private person. She didn't want to take the money from me I'd offered for her role as a tour guide. There was no way she would take money from a nosy reporter.

"I'm sorry," I said.

"Fuck you."

"Ava, I'm sorry," I said again. "I couldn't find my laptop and things were spiraling. I put two and two together. You were gone when I woke up this morning. I jumped to conclusions."

"You put two and two together and you got five," she shot back. "I went to work. I did tell you I was leaving. Your ass was asleep."

"I know," I said. "I woke up and thought you ran out on me again."

"Again?"

"The first time we had sex, you couldn't get away from me fast enough," I said. "I thought this was that. Then the laptop was gone, and shit is blowing up in New York. I just assumed you were the one who leaked the information."

"As if I give a shit about what happens in New York," she said. "I'm here because I want nothing to do with that place and the people in it. I think you think just a little too much of yourself. Maybe you are some hotshot, but I don't give a shit about you and your life there. That's not who I am. I don't get involved in drama like that. I really thought you were a bigger man. I thought you were here to leave that shit behind. You're a jerk. A vile pig. Go. Now."

"Ava, I should have talked to you," I said.

"You should have done a lot of things," she shot back. "But you didn't. You thought the little island girl with no money must be trying to screw you over. You treated me like a common whore. Like you are so special I would compromise my morals. You have a seriously inflated ego."

She was insulting me, but I deserved it. "I'm sorry," I said again.

"Sorry doesn't cut it," she said with tears flashing in her eyes. "I truly hope I will never see you again. You have the instructions for the house. Leave the keys on the counter when you run back to New York. And then lose my number. Do not book one of my rentals again. I will reject it."

She slammed the door in my face. I stared at it for several seconds. There was nothing more to say. I'd screwed up. I'd screwed up badly. She was not going to have anything to do with me. I walked to the car and headed back to the rental house. I had just destroyed the best thing that had happened to me in a really long time. I'd let my paranoia get the best of me.

I opened the door and walked straight to the charging drawer. I closed my eyes and dropped my head. I'd imploded the one relationship in my life that was good. It was the only healthy relationship I had ever really had. Granted, there were some secrets between us, but she had been so good for me. I had never felt better in my life. I had been at the highest high, and now I was at the lowest low.

I pulled out my laptop and dropped it on the counter. If I had just looked a little harder, I could have saved myself a lot of heartache. I blamed them. My family did this. As if I needed another reminder of the bullshit raining down on me, my phone started ringing again.

It was Collin. I so wanted to kick his ass. "What?" I snapped into the phone.

"Woah, what's wrong with you?" he asked.

"I know you're fucking kidding me," I said.

"I take it you've seen the news."

"No shit, Collin," I growled. "I've seen the news. Where are you?"

"Dad wants me to head up to the Hamptons," he said. "They think it best I get out of town."

"Run away from the problems once again," I said. "Wait for everyone else to fix it."

"Hey, I'm not running," he barked. "I'm just giving them what they want. They want me out of town. They think it's best if I'm not seen. They're worried someone is going to get a picture of me."

"I can't say I disagree," I said. "You should hide. Maybe do it alone. Don't take any company."

"Very funny," he said. "This was not my fault."

"It never is," I said.

"You don't have a lot of room to talk," he said.

"What the hell are you talking about?" I snapped.

"You're hiding somewhere," he said. "You're not here to deal with this."

"It's not my fucking problem to deal with!"

"Hey, I didn't do anything wrong," he said.

"I can't talk to you right now," I said. "Go hide. Run away. Wait for me and Dad to fix this. I hope like hell you have learned your lesson. You have got to stop fucking around. It's getting old. I don't know how you think you're going to make it in politics. You're going to have eyes on you everywhere you turn. Do you want to be known for the scandals or for the work you do?"

"I don't need a lecture from you," he shot back.

"You need a lecture from someone," I said. "We all should have lectured you more. Maybe we wouldn't be here now if someone had lectured you. If you would have been forced to deal with your own bullshit all these years, you might have learned a lesson. You have never been held accountable for any of your actions. It's time, Collin. This is real. You've got to get your shit together."

I hung up before I could say anything else. I loved my little brother. He was a good guy when he wasn't fucking off. Unfortunately, he fucked off a lot. He'd never really had to work a day in his life. We had been catering to him for too long. This was it. He might actually take us all down.

I barely ended the call with him when my mother called. I groaned and shook my head. I was never going to get away. "Yes, Mom," I answered.

"Did you see what that little vixen did?" she asked.

"If you mean that reporter, yes." I nodded. "I saw a few minutes of the news."

"I can't believe she's insinuating Collin killed that boy," she said. "It's disgusting. Your father is in a meeting with another lawyer. We've got lawyers coming out our ears. Lawyers for the company. Lawyers for Collin. Lawyers for the family estate. It's just a mess. Are you on your way home?"

"No, Mom," I said. "There is nothing I can do. This thing is taking on a life of its own. All I can do is take care of the company the best I can. There's little I can do to stop the media. I just talked to Collin. He said he was running to the Hamptons."

"We're having him stay at a friend's house," she said. "Your father and I will be at our house."

"Keeping your distance," I scoffed.

"Stop it," she scolded. "It's not like that. We know the press is going to follow us. That's why we're sending him to a different house. It's all very secretive. But we need you here. We need to be prepared to give a public statement. The family has to be together. Lucas has offered to be the spokesperson, but we just think it's better if we let the lawyers handle it."

"Sounds like you've got it under control," I said. "I've got to go."

"Ethan!"

I ended the call and left it at that. The worst-case scenario was coming true. The shit had hit the fan. I was used to our family being in the spotlight. We had weathered some minor scandals here and there but nothing of this magnitude. I didn't know what I could offer. In my opinion, it was best to keep a low profile and let the lawyers and PR people do their thing. If we said or did anything, it would only muddy the waters.

Chapter Twenty-Six

Ava

My head was pounding. That wasn't a good sign considering I hadn't even opened my eyes yet. I was so glad I didn't have to work at the coffee shop today. My head was not in it. I didn't have the energy to smile at anyone. I didn't feel cheery. I didn't want to wish anyone a good morning. Sulking was the only thing I wanted to do.

I tried to go back to sleep with Roxy curled up in a ball next to me. Unfortunately, my damn phone kept ringing. I reached out to grab it and saw it was my sister. I hit the decline button. She was not who I wanted to talk to. I couldn't deal with her nonsense. We had not talked in years. I didn't know why she was calling me now. There was nothing for us to talk about.

I pulled my blanket over my head and wallowed in my misery. The thing with Ethan had shaken me to my core. He'd broken me. We had shared something special. I'd given more of myself to him than any other man. For a good twenty-four hours, I had actually thought he might be the real deal. I had fantasized about him living in Oahu at least part-time. I knew he had a career in New York, but if he could work from here, it would be nice to spend time with him.

But then he went off the deep end. Because there was one person I knew I could count on, I blindly reached for my phone and pulled it into my little hideaway. I called Andrea. I partially blamed her for how shitty I felt. She'd encouraged me to go after Ethan.

"Hello," I mumbled when she answered.

"Good morning," she greeted with just a little too much enthusiasm.

"I'm mad at you," I pouted.

"Why are you mad at me?" she asked with a laugh.

"I went on that stupid date. We had sex again. I stayed the night. And guess what, he's an asshole."

"Oh no," she sighed. "What happened?"

"He's an asshole.'

"You said that," she pointed out. "What did he do? Selfish in bed?"

"No. He's just fine in that department. He's just an asshole."

I couldn't even put it into words. I was so furious with him. He had me all twisted up inside. It was a horrible feeling.

"What happened?" she asked gently.

"I went to work in the morning. I really thought we had something special. I thought we were going to have this thing, something real. I really thought he might actually be the man for me. I got home from work, and he was waiting for me. I thought we were going to spend a special day together. He freaked out. I don't know what happened. The guy lost his shit."

"Did he hurt you?" she asked.

"No, not like that," I said. "He accused me of stealing his laptop and giving the information to a reporter."

"What? Why?"

"I don't know," I said. "It was crazy. He said I took money to sell him out. It was hard to make sense of what he was saying. He truly sounded crazy. He was all over the place. Said I talked to a reporter. Asked if I knew who he really was. I don't even know what he was talking about. He insisted I was using him to get information. And the laptop. My God. He was going on and on about it. I don't know what the hell he was talking about. I'm pretty sure it was in the charging drawer."

She started laughing. "Was he drunk?"

"No." I thought about it. "I don't think so. He was just irrational. I didn't think I picked up on the crazy vibe, but now I'm not sure. He acted like I should be bowing down to him because he's this rich dude from the city."

"Did he lose his laptop?"

"I don't know!" I exclaimed. "It was like arguing with a two-year-old. I have no idea what he was freaking out about. It was just insanity. I threw him out of the house. He must have had an epiphany and realized he did put the laptop in the drawer because he came back and tried to apologize. I could give a shit. I'm done. I've taken a lot of shit in my day, but that was next level. I will not put up with that crap. He doesn't get to accuse me of some pretty horrible crimes and then just be like oops."

"I'm sorry," she said. "I thought you said he was a good guy."

"Turns out, I was wrong," I said. "He's just an asshole like everyone else."

"I'm so sorry," she said. "But at least you got to have a little fun."

"Uh, it was definitely not worth it," I said. "Now I feel like shit. I feel like I've been used. He pretended to be this amazing man, but he's just an asshole."

"Okay, that was a strike, but there are other men. Now that you've dipped your toes in the water, you are ready to start dating in earnest. Do not let one guy ruin it for you."

"I'm done," I said. "I'm so through with men. Just when you think it's safe to get in the water, you get bit. I got bit. I'm not about to get bit again."

"I'm sorry," she said. "Why don't you come out to LA? We'll go out and have some fun. Maybe you've tapped out the man market in Oahu."

"I don't know that I ever tapped into it," I said with a laugh.

"Come visit me," she said. "I miss you. It's basically the same climate. There's so much stuff to do. We can go to a concert, do some shopping, whatever."

"Thank you, but I have way too many responsibilities here," I said. I didn't tell her I didn't have the funds she did. I couldn't just buy an airline ticket and go shopping on Rodeo Drive. I wasn't the same person I had been in high school. I didn't have a credit card with no limit.

"Are you going to be okay?" she asked.

"Yes," I sighed. "I'm going to lie here sulking for a while. Tears in my beer."

"Chin up," she said. "Go get some ice cream. Watch a sad show. Cry it out, and you'll feel better in no time."

"Thanks," I said. "I'll talk to you later."

I had to walk the dogs in a bit. That meant I was going to have to leave my bed. I wasn't looking forward to it. I snuggled with Roxy a while longer before I dragged my ass out of bed and into the shower. There was a heaviness I had not experienced in a long time. I supposed I was a little spoiled. I had been enjoying a pretty carefree life in Hawaii. After losing my dad, I'd focused on being happy and living in the moment.

That just made me think about the conversation I'd had with Ethan. I told him I didn't want a relationship. I'd made it very clear I was leery of love. He convinced me it would be okay. He let me believe that there was something special between us. I should have known better. I'd let myself be swayed by a sexy smile and all the right words. He was just like so many of the men I had met in New York. It was not cool to use a broad brush to paint all the men, but it was impossible not to at this point.

Ethan had shown his true colors. I wished I would have trusted my gut. My first impression of him was right. He was a rich, city boy used to getting his own way. He saw me as an easy target. I gave him exactly what he wanted. When he was done with me, he tossed me to the side like trash.

Chapter Twenty-Seven

Ethan

"Ava, please call me back," I said.

It was the third message I'd left on her voicemail. I had texted several times, and she wasn't responding. She wasn't returning my calls. I didn't really blame her. The whole thing was my fault. I was this guy that broke down her walls and then accused her of something horrible. She had been generous with her time and herself. She'd shown me a good time. She opened her home to me and shown me some of her treasured spots on the island.

I grabbed my keys and headed to the coffee shop. I was going to keep my distance in case she decided to throw hot coffee at me. When I got to the shop, I didn't see her. I hoped she was on a break or something. I got in line and waited my turn. The woman I had seen before was at the register.

"Is Ava here?" I asked.

"Nope. She's off today."

"Thank you." I ordered a coffee I didn't want and waited. If she wasn't at the coffee shop, maybe she was home.

I took my coffee and drove to her place. Her car wasn't in the driveway. "Fuck," I hissed.

It wasn't a big island, but trying to find one person felt nearly impossible. If she wasn't working the coffee shop, there was a good chance she was walking the dogs. I didn't know where to look. I drove around her neighborhood and then slowly circled out. There were plenty of people roaming around the area, but none of them were Ava.

I gave up and drove back to the rental. I wasn't going to find her if she didn't want to be found. She wasn't going to take my calls or return my texts. It was best if I just left her alone for now. Hopefully, she would cool down and give me a chance to apologize properly.

I pulled out the laptop and opened my email. It wasn't pretty. I didn't expect anything else. I was doing my best to do damage control. It really felt like trying to plug a break in the dam with my finger. Every time I plugged one hole, something else broke open. I was replying to emails from my HR department and Legal. The Public Relations department was getting hammered. I was doing my best to help them. We were referring all inquiries to the Legal Department. I didn't know why the company had to be dragged into the mess. My people didn't do shit. Collin didn't work for the company. I didn't think he could honestly say he had ever been employed by the company. His stain was wearing off on us, and it wasn't cool.

Lucas was fighting the fires the best he could as well. My parents were in hiding as well as Collin. They were the ones skating through this while everyone else scrambled to handle the mess. It was hard not to be bitter. It was giving me serious thoughts about walking away from it all. I had my own nest egg built up. I could take my money and run. I didn't think I would be at all sad to be unemployed. My dad could take over the company or give it to Lucas for all I cared. I just wanted out.

As if Lucas sensed I was thinking about him, he called. "Hello."

"How are you?" he asked.

It was strange, but it was nice to be asked. My family just assumed this didn't bother me. No one asked me if I was doing okay with the situation. "I'm not doing great," I answered. "Pretty shitty, as a matter of fact."

"I'm sorry," he said. "I know you're sick of dealing with this bullshit. For what it's worth, I'm in your corner. I think it's bullshit you're being called back to handle your brother's affairs."

"I'm not going back," I said.

"Ever?" he laughed.

"With the way things are going, maybe," I said. "If I was in a foreign country, they might revoke my passport. Hell, I might willingly hand it over."

"I get it," he said. "Did you find your laptop?"

"Yes," I said with some embarrassment. "I freaked out for nothing. I didn't lose it. I misplaced it. Of course I figured that out after I totally blew up everything between us. I went off the rails. I accused her of all sorts of horrible things."

"Did you say her name was Ava Hunt?" he asked.

"Yes."

"I did a little digging," he said.

"It's fine," I assured him. "She doesn't know who I am. Like I said, I jumped to conclusions."

"Are you sure?" he asked. "Do you really believe she doesn't know who you are?"

"Yes," I said confidently. "She's not going to look me up. That's not like her. She doesn't care about stuff like that."

"Okay, I'm not so sure you were off base," he said.

"How so?"

"I think you need to be careful with her," he said. "She's not your friend. Her family would give just about anything to take you down. Not just you, the whole damn company. Are you absolutely sure she didn't leak the story?"

"I'm fairly confident," I said. "She doesn't know who I am."

"I think she might," he warned.

"She told me something about the Mitchells in New York had screwed over her family," I said. "But she doesn't have anything to do with them. I really don't think she cares."

"I wouldn't be so sure of that," he said.

"I don't doubt she'll figure it out eventually, but she's not going to actively research me," I insisted.

"I think you need to stay away from her," he said. "You can't afford to kick that hornet's nest. Even if she doesn't know who you are now, that doesn't mean it's going to stay that way. All it takes is one person with a camera phone that recognizes you. They see you with her, and she's dragged into this shit. Who do you think she's going to be loyal to, you or her family?"

"I don't know," I said with a laugh. "I think she hates us equally at the moment."

"Not funny," he growled. "Do you care about this woman?"

"I do. I did. I don't know."

"Do you want to see her hurt by this?" he asked. "You can't hide forever. With the way the media is picking up on this story, it's going to be huge. It's going to be running on all the national and local channels. Your picture is running right alongside Collin's. You're guilty by association. Hell, I think I've seen your face more in the last day than the twenty years I've known you. It's only a matter of time before someone spots you. Once that happens, the press is going to be on you. You're not going to escape. If you're around her, she's pulled in."

"Fucking Collin," I hissed.

"Look, I don't have to tell you the board is pretty antsy right now," he said.

"What have you heard?"

"A couple of rumors are floating," he said hesitantly.

"Like?"

"Like it might save the company to vote you out," he said.

I should have been more upset than I was. I didn't want to be pushed out of the company, but if I was, I couldn't muster the sadness. It was what I had thought about doing. "Because of this?" I asked.

"Because this is one in a long line of scandals the company has been attached to," he said. "I've told them if they vote you out, that's it. Stocks will plummet, and the company will be done. There are always bigger sharks out there. One of the companies chomping at our heels will show up. They already smell blood in the water. They're circling. They'll take us down bit by bit."

"I can't let that happen," I said. "My grandfather started the company, and I'm going to lose it on my watch?"

"I'm just telling you what's going on here," he said. "If the board votes and you are removed, people are going to lose a lot of money. That's just more bad press for you. The more your face is splashed all over the TV, the higher the risk Ava figures out who you are. All it's going to take is one news clip and it's over. Do you think you can trust her not to tell the press where you are?"

"I don't know."

"There are just so many things that could go wrong with this scenario," he said. "I know you've got the hots for her, but this is just a bad idea. You need to keep your distance."

"I wonder what it costs to get a new identity," I mused aloud.

"Not funny."

"Don't you ever think about just running away?" I asked.

"Not since I was five," he replied.

"Okay," I said. "I'll leave her alone. I'm still in her house. At this point, I think it would be more of a risk to try and move to a hotel. Someone is bound to recognize the name. I think it's better if I just lay low."

"Good plan," he said. "I guess it might be better if you stay there."

"I'm sorry you're having to carry so much of this burden," I told him. "My family owes you big."

"I'm just doing my part," he said. "My ass in on the line, too. If the board does call a vote and I go against them, you can be sure I'll be removed and they'll just call another vote."

"Quietly ask around and see what everyone is thinking," I said. "I'm not looking to go up against a mutiny. Does my dad know?"

"Yes," he answered. "You know him. He's making all kinds of threats."

"Fuck," I groaned again. "All right. I'm going to get with Legal and see what happens next. I might see if I can take a leave of absence. That'll satisfy the board and give the story time to die down."

"I hope that'll work," he said.

"Have you heard anything more about the guy that died?" I asked. "Are his parents speaking out?"

"Not yet," he said. "But again, there's blood in the water. When Mitchell money is involved, there are plenty of people with their hands out hoping to get a piece of the action. From what I understand, your brother's lawyers are preparing him for a civil suit."

I blew out a breath. "It just keeps getting better and better."

"Sorry," he said. "I wish I had better news. Try and relax. I know you won't but try."

"Thanks."

I ended the call and moved to look out over the deck. This was a slow train crash happening before my very eyes, and I was helpless to stop it. I was torn between wanting to say fuck it all and jumping in to fight the fire. There wasn't much I could do to kill the story, but I could come out swinging. Yes, Collin had fucked up, but it had zero to do with the company.

I thought about Ava. I had been trying to mend fences with her, but it didn't matter. I couldn't be with her. Ever. She deserved an apology, but I couldn't give it because that would mean she and I would be acquainted again. I had to leave her alone. I couldn't go to dinner with her or have pancakes together. It sucked to have to give up the one person I was certain I could have spent the rest of my life with.

And then there was my family. It was just the wrong time. The wrong names. Even though it felt right, it was wrong.

Chapter Twenty-Eight

Ava

I woke up feeling better than I had in a week. I knew time healed all wounds. This wound felt like it was infected. Ethan had called the first day and then disappeared. The only reason I knew he was still around was because he was in my rental house. I had begged Richard to go by the house and make sure it was still standing. Although Ethan had apologized, he had been pretty unhinged that day. I didn't know if he had decided I'd stolen something else and went all scorched earth. I was a little concerned he would burn my house down or something equally crazy.

The entire week had been full of anger and hurt and then sadness. I was actually surprised to be feeling so shitty after he dumped me. It wasn't like we were married or even in a committed relationship. We'd hooked up a couple times and shared some meals. So what we went surfing and hiking together. That didn't mean shit. He wasn't even a friend. He was just some dude I'd fucked around with.

I hated that I couldn't just dismiss him. At the coffee shop, I found myself constantly looking for him in line. I don't know what I would have done if he'd shown up. I probably would have shouted him right out of the damn place. I didn't actually want to see him.

I didn't understand how I let one man screw with my head so badly. I knew his type. He represented everything I hated. He was the kind of guy I typically ran away from. There were plenty of his type that showed up in Oahu thinking they were all that and a bag of chips. I had never been attracted to them. Sometimes they flirted with me, but usually my cold shoulder kept them at bay. Ethan was just another one of them.

He was so much like the guys I'd dated in college. He was a little older, but it was good to see they never changed. I considered myself lucky for dodging that bullet. I could have ended up with one of them. They would have turned into men like Ethan. They were all about themselves. They couldn't believe people did things just to be nice. There was always an angle. To think I would stoop so low to sell information about him was the most insulting accusation.

I was glad he was out of my life but sad that he was gone. Somehow, in the short amount of time we were together, he'd burrowed into my heart. I couldn't seem to get rid of him. I kept telling myself it wasn't real. There was nothing to feel sad about losing because it had never been real. We had never been a couple. I couldn't have feelings for a man I didn't truly know.

But today felt a little different. I wasn't as sad. I was lonely and maybe bummed, but I didn't feel like crying. In fact, I felt like getting out of the apartment and into the water. I wanted a new challenge. I dressed and headed out to do some surfing. I rode wave after wave. It was hard not to associate surfing with him, but the more I did it without him, the less I would think about him. I was going to have to revisit all the places I had taken him. Then it wouldn't be the last time I was there he was with me.

Roxy and I would re-christen all our favorite spots and exorcise his presence from them. If she was a boy, she could hike her leg and piss all over the place to eliminate his scent. The time on the beach helped. I was healing once again. Another heartbreak in the books. I just hoped I'd learned a lesson. The next time I saw a man that looked anything like Ethan or was from New York, I was going in the opposite direction. I wasn't even going to give him a chance to convince me he was good. Clearly, I would fall for just about anything. My best option was to abstain from city boys.

I was going to find myself a good Navy man. I was always getting asked out when I worked at the coffee shop. The next guy that asked me out, I was going to say yes. That would further remove Ethan from my memory. I wasn't sure I was going to be falling into bed with any of them, but maybe. That was going to be something else I had to do again. Was it crazy I didn't want sex with anyone else? Maybe I could get hypnotized. If they could help people quit smoking, they could help me quit Ethan.

When I got home, Roxy was waiting on the couch for me. "Hey girl," I said and kissed her nose. "I'm going to shower and then we'll go for a walk."

I washed the sea from my hair and dressed for the walk with Roxy. She had been my rock as usual. She was my shoulder to lean on. She was a hell of a lot softer than a shoulder. I grabbed her leash, which sent her into a tailspin. She spun around and yipped while I attempted to attach it.

I took her on a long walk. I was trying to wear us both out. The fresh air did me good. I would have stayed out all day, but I did have to give some attention to my rental property business. I needed to do my books for the month and check to see if I had any requests. I was still waiting for the house to get another renter. So far, I had nothing un-til the spring. I wanted to ask Ethan to leave a review, but there was no way. My pride wouldn't allow it. I wasn't asking him for a damn thing.

I returned home, fed and watered Roxy, and then sat down at the kitchen table to go over the books. I happened to notice I had a missed call from a number I didn't recognize. There were a few inquiries about the condo. I assumed the call was probably from a potential renter and called it back.

"Hello? Ava? Is that you?"

I sat in stunned silence when the person picked up. I recognized the voice. It was a voice I didn't care to hear. I considered hanging up.

"Don't hang up," Jenny said. "I have to talk to you."

I sighed, knowing I was caught. My sister had been bugging me nonstop. "What do you want, Jenny?"

"I'm in trouble," she said in a small voice. "Serious trouble."

"And you're calling me?" I asked with frustration.

"Yes," she said. "I need help. I'm in deep shit."

"I'm sure you can call one of your rich friends," I said. "I'm sure there is a rich relative you can shake out of our family tree if you look hard enough."

"Ava, please," she said. "This is real. I'm in deep."

"Let me guess, it involves a guy," I said dryly.

"Yes."

I shook my head. Jenny had gone off the rails a long time ago. She was four years younger than I was, but it was like we were raised by different people. In a way, I guess we were. I had gotten four extra years with our dad when we were little. He had been a grounding force. When my mom took us away, Jenny had been very young. She'd been raised with the wolverines that were my mother's family. They'd molded her into one of them.

"I don't know why you are calling me," I said. "I can't help you."

"I don't know who else to call," she said.

"Funny, when Dad was dying and I was buried under a mountain of debt, I called you for help," I said. "You couldn't help me. You couldn't help your own father. You were too busy with your own life. You were partying and hooking up with guys. That was more important than saying goodbye to your father or using even a penny of your inheritance to help. I knew who to call back then, and you shut me down."

"That was a mistake," she blurted out. "I'm sorry, but this is different. I could be in real trouble here, Ava. I don't have the connections anymore."

"You got yourself into trouble again," I said. "Although I'm not sure you ever got yourself out of trouble."

"You're right," she said. "I've made a lot of mistakes. You're my sister, Ava. You're all I have left."

"I haven't even talked to you in years," I said. "What makes you think you have me? You abandoned me a long time ago."

"You're better than that," she said. "I need help. You're the only person I could call."

"No, I'm the only person left to call," I corrected. "I'm guessing you've called everyone else on your contact list, and nobody will help you."

"That's not true!"

"What do you want, Jenny?" I sighed. "I don't have any money. Anytime you're in trouble, it costs money to get you out of it. I think you're just going to have to ride this one out on your own. You do the crime, you do the time."

"That would be funny if I wasn't actually looking at time," she shot back.

That got my attention. "Are you serious?" I asked.

"Unfortunately, I am," she said. "The guy I was seeing got me into some trouble. He's got money and a powerful family. He's going to be fine, but I think they are trying to pin the blame on me. I don't know how to fight this. I didn't do anything."

I shook my head. It had been the same story with her for as long as I could remember. I was her big sister. Once upon a time, we had been close. Those days were long gone, but the sister bond really never went away.

"I'm sorry, Jenny," I said. "I think you're on your own. I don't have any way to help you. This was bound to happen one day. I don't wish you ill will, but you have to learn sometime. No one is going to save you except yourself. Only you can fix whatever it is you broke. My advice would be own up to the mistake and ask for forgiveness. If it's legal trouble, ask for a plea deal. If I were you, I would take this as a wakeup call. It's time to learn. It's time to grow up. We don't have family that will bail us out. When Dad was sick, I learned that. It's a sink or swim situation. You can choose to fight like hell and swim, or sink. Goodbye."

I ended the call and blocked the number. I felt guilty for abandoning her, but there was nothing I could do. Jenny loved rich guys. She wanted back into that lifestyle. Hooking up with rich guys was how she was holding on to that life. Her main goal in life was to marry rich. It wasn't exactly a savvy plan, but it was her choice. She wasn't picky about her men. She'd been in some bad positions because she didn't ask questions. She saw money and jumped. She'd been involved in a very ugly divorce as the other woman.

I thought that would have been her come to Jesus moment. It wasn't. She just kept looking for the next guy. I blamed my mother for encouraging such behavior. Jenny was a beautiful, smart girl and could have really done something with her life. Instead, our mother had taught her money and looks were the most important things in a man. They were the most important things in life. She was paying a high price for our mother's shitty parenting.

There were days I missed Jenny like crazy. But then I realized I missed the relationship Jenny and I had, not the person she was today. I couldn't support her decisions, and I sure as hell did not want to get dragged into one of her messes. I had built a life I was proud of. That was my priority. Jenny was on her own.

THE END

TOUCH THE SEA BOOK TWO
Gentle
rhythm
bestselling author
autumn gaze

Touch the Sea Series

Book 1 – Seduction Island
Book 2 – Gentle Rhythm
Book 3 – Dancing on Waves
Book 4 – Stormy Waters
Book 5 – Tempting the Ocean

Wicked Fates Series

Book 1 – Beautiful Darkness
Book 2 – Twisted Darkness
Book 3 – Wicked Darkness

Find Autumn Gaze:

Autumn Gaze Newsletter:
https://www.autumngaze.com/sign-up
Autumn Gaze Facebook Page:
https://www.facebook.com/AutumnGazeAuthor
Autumn Gaze Website:
http://www.autumngaze.com

Want to read more...

FREE BOOKS?

Sign up for Autumn's newsletter
And she'll send you updates on new releases, ARC copies of books
and a whole lotta fun!
Sign up for news and updates!
https://www.autumngaze.com/sign-up[1]

---

1. https://l.facebook.com/l.php?u=https%3A%2F%2Fwww.autumngaze.com%2Fsign-up%3Ffb-clid%3DIwAR19Pln3ibiSJ3sbPjqwZi2C2ouEk0HNj3WPfqfFHOACbgTxP-nyPseA8z2I&h=AT2zXnGSz1iKPMdJCv3D1jaSfPpsk9GF78_lcDB8lQuthwcLpds-du_0dX1lpDVC_R_aw9eie2R8y7wQzGrIpKgoi-6TEh8H8t1IcDKGEJ-NzgaLtedWWgkAd-PDYhWUrxkU

More by Autumn Gaze

Department of Defense

Dead Ahead
Blue Falcon
Joint Service
Indirect Attack
Book Trailer:
https://lumen5.com/user/lexy-timms/dead-ahead-trailer-l12dn/[1]

---

1. https://l.facebook.com/l.php?u=https%3A%2F%2Flumen5.com%2Fuser%2Flexy-timms%2Fdead-ahead-trailer-
l12dn%2F%3Ffbclid%3DIwAR0LhBM3pT9aIz8DEG5FXeXsDrBzasZgjxKC6RXAoj-
yP8niyxJHcfLGE_o&h=AT2jwhb69pufcA2B8U84he2HH7eSLXUodpU-
gOLs5q6X6DES914B03gx4E9QEWM8qS9YJJpajWAAa9yWDp1Ha2ExKlr1ICtVEhiTQ1NRqL-
gY6naiPq1OCugPceon3NwSkXZM

Don't miss out!

Visit the website below and you can sign up to receive emails whenever Autumn Gaze publishes a new book. There's no charge and no obligation.

https://books2read.com/r/B-A-RKRU-ROFDC

Connecting independent readers to independent writers.

Did you love *Seduction Island*? Then you should read *Dead Ahead*[2] by Lexy Timms and Autumn Gaze!

The only easy day was yesterday...

Tri:

I'm a Navy SEAL on a mission to find out what's happening in a politically-charged environment. When things go horribly wrong, I find myself saddled with my exact opposite: a female scientist who never runs out of questions or words. Now we're stuck on a deserted island with no way off and information vital to avoiding World War III. Will we make it off the island in time to warn the world what's coming? And will we do it with our hearts still intact?

Ashley:

---

2. https://books2read.com/u/bOzByo

3. https://books2read.com/u/bOzByo

They sent me to an island to find out why the marine life off the coast was behaving strangely. The only problem? It's a contested land inhabited by terrorists. When I find myself stranded on the island with a Navy SEAL who saved my life, I don't know whether we'll make it off alive. But one thing I do know? I might be falling for the man with the haunting blue eyes. Before we find out whether we have a future together, we have to escape terrorists, get off the island, and save the world.

Department of Defense Series:

Dead AheadBlue FalconJoint ServiceIndirect Attack

Also by Autumn Gaze

Department of Defense Series
Dead Ahead
Blue Falcon
Joint Service
Indirect Attack

Touch the Sea Series
Seduction Island

Wicked Fates Series
Beautiful Darkness
Twisted Darkness
Wicked Darkness

Watch for more at www.autumngaze.com.

About the Author

Autumn Gaze writes stories about love and life. She grew up reading every book she could get her hands on and still loves reading and watching movies. Stay tuned for more news to come!

She is joining USA Today Bestselling Author, Lexy Timms, on a few collaborated series and can't wait to share the Department of Defense Contemporary romance series with readers!

Read more at www.autumngaze.com.